# THE TRUTH KILLS

## BOOK ONE OF THE TRUTH KILLS TRIOLOGY

## SEAN LA'MONT

**Cover Design and Art by Sean La'Mont**
**Edited and Publishing Assistance by Michelle Morrow, M.S., Publishology**

# Contents

*I dedicate this book to my Lord and Savior.*
*Though you are not the focal point of this book, you are the Most*
*High in my life. I owe everything to you. Thank you for all the*
*wonderful gifts and blessings you have bestowed upon me.*
*I wholeheartedly pray that each day, all that I create will bring*
*praise to your Holy name.*

# THE TRUTH KILLS

# ONE

"How did he find out?" She asked herself repeatedly as tears poured from her blackened eyes. Nicole had only lived in Atlanta for thirteen months, and the truth once again threatened her life. *I can't stop trembling. How did he find out? No one in the entire state of Georgia knows the truth about me. This is the main reason I decided to relocate to Atlanta.* "What the hell is wrong with me?" she cried.

The speedometer read 79—way above the posted speed limit. *I need to slow down; the last thing I need is an officer of the law in my business.* A quick glance in the rearview put her at ease to discover that he wasn't following her.

Street lamps along the interstate briefly illuminated the car's interior.

A flash of light revealed her swollen, blackened eyes.

She worried about what other injuries he had inflicted upon her. The taste of blood was fresh in her mouth.

*I just don't understand why the man I believed to have loved me so much would try to kill me. I do know I am thankful to have escaped with my life.*

Glancing down, she noticed her pink, blood-stained bra visible through her torn dress. *I hate myself. I can hear my father laughing at me.*

She desperately fought back the emotional breakdown that threatened to consume her. "Keep driving," she told herself, even though she had no idea where she was going.

*Maybe I should have let him kill me. I know I've lost everything, anyway. I want to die.* It had been years since she felt this way. *Why do I even try? Is this life worth what I go through?* She cried. *Where am I going? I can't go to a friend's house. How can I explain my current condition? What if he calls everyone we know? What am I going to do?* Her thoughts raced frantically as she drove her pink Lexus through Atlanta.

# Two

He noticed Isaiah's work truck parked awkwardly in the driveway and partially on the lawn. He peered into the garage and saw that Nicole's Lexus was gone as he casually walked up to the front door. He rang the doorbell.

He wondered out loud to himself, "Why isn't Isaiah at work?"

No answer. He rang again. No answer.

"Yo, Isaiah, it's Malik," he yelled into the door. Malik pounded on the door with his fist. "Isaiah!"

Malik walked around the left side of the modern two-story home. He walked up the small wooden steps to the open patio deck. He banged loudly on the heavy sliding glass door.

"Isaiah, it's Malik!"

Isaiah is startled awake. "Who is it?" he asked groggily.

"Isaiah!" Malik pounded on the glass again.

"Hold on, man!" Isaiah unhurriedly rose from the black leather couch. He winced from a severe headache. He fumbled with the latch on the sliding glass door and reluctantly opened it for Malik.

Isaiah helplessly collapsed back onto the couch, away from Malik. "What's up, Malik?"

"What happened to you and Nicole for dinner last night? Either one of you could have called and let us know you weren't coming. Y'all didn't even have the decency to answer your phones. I started driving by last night to see what the hell was going on. Michelle is mad as hell. It ain't like y'all to miss Michelle's cooking. You know the boys look forward to Nicole's bedtime stories." He stood over Isaiah.

Isaiah groaned. He simply wanted to be left alone. He didn't feel like talking.

"I know you hear me. What the hell is wrong with you? Why you ain't you at work?"

Isaiah groaned again.

"Where's Nicole?" Malik asked. "Is she at the gallery? Michelle said she had to meet the security system installers today. Why is it so damn dark in here?"

Malik pulled open the floor-length vertical blinds. "Open this shit up and let some light in here."

He noticed that the huge framed professional portrait of Isaiah and Nicole, which usually hung over the large entertainment center, had shattered in the foyer against the front door. There were numerous destroyed frames and glass.

"What the hell happened up in here? Did y'all have a fight or something?"

Malik saw an empty brandy bottle on the coffee table. He leaned over Isaiah. "Damn, you stink. Did you swim in the shit? Hey?" He slapped Isaiah's feet.

"I don't feel like talking, man," Isaiah responded.

"You aw'ight?" Malik asked.

"Just let it go, man."

"Let what go?" He sat at the end of the couch, prodding Isaiah's feet. "Did y'all have a fight or something? What's up?"

"I told you I don't want to talk about it."

"Y'all did have a fight. It's about time." Malik couldn't believe it. He had never even seen them disagree before. "What the hell did Heathcliff and Claire Huxtable fight about?" He laughed.

Isaiah sat up on the couch, lowered his head, and buried his face in his huge hands.

"Dawg, it ain't that bad, she'll be back," Malik assured him.

"No, she won't," Isaiah said matter-of-factly as he faced Malik.

"Got damn, she fucked you up!" Malik yelled, looking at the deep scratches on his eyes, face, and neck. "What the hell did you do?"

"I tried to kill her, man." Isaiah's eyes filled with tears. "I was so fuckin' mad."

Malik leaped from his seat. "You tried to kill her? Nicole? What?"

Isaiah wiped his eyes with his hands.

"Hey man, this is some serious shit, you need to start talking right now. What the fuck happened?" Malik insisted.

Isaiah stared directly into Malik's eyes. He slowly stood up, reached for the coffee table, and handed Malik a large manila envelope. "Page seventeen."

# THREE

Nicole Bennett is awakened to the ringing of her cell phone. Her eyes opened as her head and body were engulfed with pain.

She couldn't recollect where she was.

Her face throbbed with pain. She blindly reached across the bed and fumbled on the nightstand for her phone. She seized her phone and brought it to her face to see who was calling.

Her right eye was swollen shut. It was him.

It all came back to her now.

*What could he possibly have to say to me? Maybe he's calling to see if I have survived his brutal attack. He might be calling to inform me that all my belongings are strewn across the front yard.*

She decided to turn off her cell phone.

She knew Isaiah better than that. She had never seen Isaiah angry before, especially when that anger was directed at her. She shuddered at how close to death she had been. Guilt and self-pity devoured her. She cried. Deep, heart-wrenching wails filled the silent room. She cried so hard that she found it difficult to breathe as she completely surrendered to her emotions.

She finally took a deep breath to collect herself. She didn't care anymore. She was tired of her life. She wanted out. She thought about all she had forfeited to become the woman she is today. She gave away her family, her innocence, and most importantly, her self-respect. She wanted to lie in this bed and never wake up again. She cried herself back to sleep.

Nicole reawakened at 9:49 A.M. She sluggishly sat up and reached for her purse on the nightstand.

The room was dark, with the heavy drapes hanging over the motel room windows.

She reached inside her purse and seized the small bottle of aspirin.

She turned on the archaic brown lamp. The bright light hurt her eye.

She pulled the cheap, faded old comforter off her sore body. With great effort, she managed to place both legs over the side of the bed. She was completely drained and extremely weak. She knew she had to make it to the bathroom.

She surveyed the typical, basically furnished motel room. She assumed the bathroom sat around the corner at the end of the wall. Nicole stood up slowly as she steadied herself against the wall. She carefully walked toward the bathroom on the coarse motel carpet. As she made the corner, she turned on the light switch. She faced the mirror; her hands instinctively covered her mouth as she released a muffled scream. She dropped the bottle of aspirin into the sink as she almost fainted; she barely caught hold of the sink. She forced herself to stand again as tears filled her eyes.

She gasped at her own reflection.

Her entire face had been severely beaten, and now both eyes were black. Her right eye is swollen shut. The left side of her mouth, where her lips connected, is severed and purplish with dried blood. Her nose appeared to be twice its normal size. Her entire face was swollen, and several spots of dried blood covered her cheeks.

She reached for one of the plastic cups on the counter near the

sink, and she noticed her naked hand and recollected that he forcefully removed her engagement ring. She let the water run until it
became hot and filled her cup. She took three aspirins.

She noticed her pink, blood-stained bra. She returned to the
main room to examine the rest of her body in front of the mirror
connected to the desk. Her body was littered with bruises and
scratches.

She sat on the edge of the bed and began to rub her legs.

*How did he find out?* That question really puzzled her. In that
instant, she remembered her cell phone.

She quickly turned it on.

After a few minutes, her phone audibly indicated that she had
new messages. She looked at the screen, which displayed that she
had six missed calls.

Nicole pressed the call voice-mail button. She held the phone
to her ear. Her heartbeat felt so powerful that it seemed to pulse
throughout the entire room.

"You have five new messages and three saved messages," the
phone chirped.

"New message: "Girl, where y'all at? Dinner has been ready for
over an hour. Malik just fed the kids. I don't think they're coming.
Something must have happened."

Nicole had totally forgotten about dinner. She knew she had
to call Michelle to apologize and explain. *Oh my gosh. What if he
told Michelle?* She had bigger problems to deal with. She pressed 7
to delete the call.

"Your message has been deleted. Press 1."

"New message."

She heard heavy breathing, and the line went dead.

"To replay this message, press 1. To delete this message, press 7.
To call the message center, press 8. To save this message, press 9."

Nicole pressed 7.

"Your message has been deleted. To undelete, press 1."

"New message," the phone continued.

"Fuck you. Did you understand that? I said fuck you." He spoke slowly and deliberately, making sure to enunciate each syllable with perfect inebriated dialect. "You hear me?" He laughed. "You happy now? You selfish mutha-fucka. One question, you couldn't tell me the truth about you before I fucked you bitch? Before I fell in love with you and asked you to marry me bitch? Before we built this life together bitch? Fuck you bitch!"

Nicole pressed 7.

She felt a new wave of guilt wash over her.

"Message deleted. To undelete, press 1. New message..."

She could hear him laughing crazily in the background.

"This is fucking comedy, all the time you got me to open up about myself with your honesty bullshit, and you ain't said shit. I wish I had killed your bitch ass." The impact of his words hurt more than his fists.

"Message deleted. To undelete this message, press 1."

"New message."

"Answer your fuckin' phone bitch, you hear me? Answer your phone. You need to come and get all your shit and get the fuck outta my life, now."

Nicole pressed 7.

"Message deleted. To undelete this message, press 1."

"End of messages."

She fell backwards onto the bed, looking at the ceiling, letting her cell phone fall from her hands. She pressed her palms to her forehead.

*What the hell is wrong with me? I should have told him from the beginning; he had a right to know. I just couldn't tell him. He would have never wanted to see me again, let alone marry me.*

Nicole was in deep thought when the motel phone rang.

She sat up straight and stared at the phone in disbelief. *There is no way he knows I'm here.* She seized the motel phone and hesitantly held the receiver to her ear.

"Hello?" she answered cautiously.

"Good morning, this is Brian, the front desk clerk."

She heard his light southern accent.

"I hope that you are feeling better this morning."

She didn't remember him.

"I'm alive," Nicole responded, trying her best to picture his face. Her speech is impaired because of the injury to her mouth.

"You scared me to death coming in here like that last night. I tried to call the police, and you stopped me. You asked me to help you. I immediately put you in a room. I told you to try to get a good night's rest, and you handed me your car keys."

"Thank you so much, Brian, for your help," she interrupted. "I don't have much cash, but I have several credit cards. I can..."

"That's not why I'm calling you. I'm sorry I didn't get your name."

"Nicole. Nicole Bennett."

"Miss Bennett, you are not even registered in this motel. I figured whoever did that to you may be out to find you. You can stay here as long as you need to."

"Thank you for your hospitality, but I think I'm okay," she lied.

"I'm about to eat. What would you like for breakfast?"

"You have already done so much for me, I couldn't."

"Please, I haven't eaten yet anyway. So, what would you like to eat?" He insisted.

"Anything edible will be just fine, thank you."

"And what would you like to drink?"

"Water, please, I'm really thirsty."

"See you in about 15, 20 minutes, okay?"

"Please give me half an hour to clean myself up, I don't want to scare you again." It hurt for her to smile. She did remember him.

"Miss Bennett, I don't want you to get the wrong impression about me. I'm just trying to help."

"Please call me Nicole."

"Okay, Nicole, I want you to know that you can feel

completely safe with me. I would never try to take advantage of you, given all you have been through. I mean, I'm just trying to put you at ease, so if it helps you to know, I'm gay. I'm only telling you this because you probably aren't very trusting of men right now."

"I already knew that, see you in half an hour. And Brian, thank you." Nicole replaced the receiver.

# FOUR

"What the hell is this?" Malik asked, holding up the envelope.

"Take the magazine out of the envelope," Isaiah instructed. "I want you to see it just like I did."

"I don't want to read no damn magazine." He stood up. "What the fuck happened?" Malik removed the magazine from the envelope.

"Page seventeen." Isaiah sat on the loveseat, anticipating Malik's reaction.

He read the cover. "*Southern California Connections*, what kind of shit is this?"

"That's the same thing that I said." Malik opened the magazine to page four.

Numerous advertisements with photos featuring nude and semi-nude females covered the pages. Underneath the photos are titles and brief descriptions of what the females are offering.

"This is what all the bullshit is about? You tried to kill her for selling pussy? So, what, she was a ho. So, we were, except we were stupid, we did it for free?" Malik read the date on the cover. "Man, this shit is over four years old. How you going to trip over something she did before she met you?"

"Page seventeen, Malik," Isaiah instructed, waiting patiently for him to discover the truth.

Malik found page seventeen, and right before his very eyes, was a large color photo of a scantily clad Nicole titled, "SEEING IS BELIEVING."

He noticed she was slightly thinner in this picture with a different name. "Man, you tried to kill this? You're a damn fool," Malik laughed.

"Read it."

"Seeing is believing," Malik read aloud. "Beautiful, passable, 26-year-old, pre-op transsexual... Transsexual!! With ten and a half functional inches of pleasure?!!"

Malik threw the magazine to the floor in shock. "What the fuck? Aw hell naw!! Nicole got a dick, nigga?!"

"Hell no, Nicole ain't got no dick!! You know I don't get down like that," Isaiah said as he stood up to face Malik.

"I just thought." Malik threw up his hands as if surrendering.

"You thought wrong, fool."

"That's some nasty, fucked-up shit. Aw hell naw!"

"Now you know how I felt." Isaiah found relief in Malik's reaction.

"That's some nasty, RuPaul, chick wit-a dick, kill a nigga type shit. I'm sorry, Dawg, I can't believe that shit." Malik sat on the couch. "That shit ain't right, you alright man?"

"Hell no, I ain't alright," Isaiah said as he reclaimed his spot on the loveseat.

"Where did you get that fucked up magazine?"

"It was sitting on my desk in that manila envelope with page seventeen written on it. After I read it, I sat at my desk in shock, then I got mad as hell. I confronted everybody in the shop; no one knew what I was talking about."

"I can't believe that shit, I would have never guessed in a million years." Malik understood why Isaiah attempted to kill Nicole. To find out that your fiancée was born male. He knew how much Isaiah loved Nicole and what she meant to him. Malik placed himself in Isaiah's shoes and really felt his pain. "So, what did you say? What did you do?"

"I prayed it was a lie. I walked in the house; she ran down the stairs in a rush to get to your house for dinner. She could tell I was upset from my facial expressions. She ran up on me and tried to touch me. I pushed her hands away from me. I threw the manila envelope at her, and we said some shit. Then I said, 'Fuck it, are you a man?'"

Isaiah stood up for emphasis. "She acted like she didn't hear me. So, I asked her ass again. Are you a mutha-fuckin' man? She stepped back, then started crying. That's when I knew the truth. Talking shit about do I look like a man? Do I act like a man? Do I feel like a man when you're making love to me?"

"Well, did she?" Malik asked innocently.

Isaiah towered over Malik. "I'll whip your mutha- fuckin' ass."

"Dawg, you trippin,' I just asked you a question." Malik defended. "When you first got with Nicole, we were all drooling. All our girls were hating, especially my Michelle. And as we all got to know her, she became one of the family. This is going to kill Michelle."

"Don't tell Michelle shit. You're the only person that knows, and whoever left that shit on my desk."

"Isaiah, we go way back. I would never put you out like that."

"Thanks, man." They touched fists.

He sat next to Malik on the couch. "I just want that faggot out of my life. I hate that bitch."

"I hear you, Dawg." His opinion of Nicole had drastically changed. Before this startling revelation, Malik was quite fond of Nicole. Watching the two of them interact led him to believe they were made for each other. They were inseparable. They did everything together. The way they looked at each other made it easy to visualize the love they shared. He felt really bad for Isaiah.

"Finally, you meet the woman of your dreams and find out it's all an illusion." Malik unexpectedly hated Nicole, too. "I'm sitting here in disbelief. How could she do that to you?"

"She? She's a fucking man," Isaiah yelled as he began to pace back and forth.

"Let's put it this way, she, him, shim, whatever. She definitely ain't no man now. I'm damn sure I have never seen a man look like Nicole. It's even hard for me to call her, him. That's some fucked up shit."

"I didn't even think about going back to the penitentiary for murder. I just wanted that bitch dead. If you found out your wife was born a dude, you wouldn't trip?"

"I don't know if I would have tried to kill her, but I would start fucking her in the ass." He laughed, trying to break the tension. "No, seriously, I couldn't honestly say what I would do. I honestly couldn't imagine life without Michelle. Can I ask you something, man?"

"What's up?"

"Seriously...the pussy? Couldn't you tell? I remember the first time you hit it; you called and said it was fire. It didn't feel... different?"

Isaiah walked around the coffee table in deep thought as he evaluated Malik's question. "To be honest, I was so happy to finally get the pussy. Man, I could have been fucking her armpit and thought it was fire. I guess it was pussy; hot, wet, and real tight. I busted a nut."

"That's probably because the pussy was brand new."

"Now that I think about it, when we first started fucking, it was extremely uncomfortable for both of us. It was a little tight, but I opened it up, and now it's straight. I ain't never been big on eating pussy, and she wasn't into that. So, I can't tell you if it really looked or tasted different. She said she had problems with her reproductive organs due to an accident she suffered as a child."

"What accident?" Malik asked.

"You remember, I told you she couldn't have children because of the accident, when we first met. I didn't mind because I already have a son. She said she lost both of her parents, and her pelvis was crushed in that accident. She had to have some kind of reconstructive surgery so she could urinate and have sex. She's a fucking liar, man. I wonder what else she lied to me about. Did she really love me, or was that a lie? How can you straight out lie to the one you claim you love?"

"Now you know she loved your funny-looking, monkey ass. I single-handedly give Nicole credit for the man you are today. She took the one thing you do well and turned it into a successful business. I mean all aspects of your business, from marketing to accounting. She upgraded your life to a whole new status."

"I wanted my wife to be a real fuckin' woman."

"He is a real fuckin' woman," Malik laughed.

"Man, don't play with me." He sat on the matching love seat. "Remember, when I first met her, I told you it was something different about this girl. Different from all the other females I have ever been with, including my baby's mama. The way she carries herself, her cool ass personality, her intelligence, and classiness. It all makes sense now. That's why she was so freaky. She would let me fuck her in the ass. Suck my dick for breakfast, lunch, and dinner. How long was she a ho? She could have contracted AIDS."

"Before I married Michelle, we were the biggest hoes in Atlanta. We were fucking so many different women, we started taking Viagra. You remember that shit."

"You can't turn no ho into a housewife."

"Hell, I did. Michelle ain't never confessed to being a prostitute, but the way she empties my dick, she obviously did something in her past." Malik smiled.

"So, what do I do now?" Isaiah asked as he massaged his temples.

"Have you heard from her?"

"I tried calling her all night. I left at least four messages. Where is she? Did I put her in the hospital? She could be lying dead somewhere. I might have killed her for real." Isaiah panicked, reliving the ten years he served in prison for drug trafficking in Florida. "She could be telling the cops that I tried to kill her."

"Isaiah, chill the fuck out, maybe she's called Michelle. Where's the phone?"

"I think it's on the couch."

Malik found the cordless housephone on the couch and dialed his wife's work number.

"Man, watch what you say," Isaiah advised Malik.

"I got this. You just chill the fuck out."

Michelle answered. "Hello, and thank you for calling Universal Insurance. This is Michelle Reed in Collections; how may I help you?"

"Hey, baby, you sound so professional. Daddy's so proud of Mama."

"Hi, Poo-Poo," Michelle cooed quietly into the phone. "You're up early. Have you heard from Nicole and Isaiah?"

"I'm over here now."

"Was anyone there? I know Nicole had to meet the security company for installation at the gallery, and Isaiah should be at work."

"Isaiah is home."

"Is Nicole there? Let me speak to Nicole."

"No, she's at the gallery," Malik lied.

"Why is Isaiah at home, and what happened to them having Sunday dinner with us last night? No, let him tell me that. Put Isaiah on the phone."

Malik covered the receiver with his hand. "Man, she wants to talk with you."

Isaiah shook his head no.

"You know what, baby? Isaiah is sick," he lied again as he winked at Isaiah.

"And you're still there? You hate it when people are sick. You won't even stay in the same room with us in your own house. So why are you lying to me, Malik Jovan Reed?"

"Baby, they got into a fight, and he doesn't feel like talking right now." He winked at Isaiah again.

"They got into a fight?! About what?" Michelle realized that she was getting loud. "They never fight," she whispered into the phone.

"He won't tell me," Malik lied again. "Isaiah wants to know if you have heard from her?"

"What!" She regained composure. "Have I heard from her? Where is she? She wasn't at the gallery when I called her this morning. I called her cell phone and left her a message. It's not like Nicole not to answer her phone. When did she leave?"

"I don't know, he didn't tell me."

"Put Isaiah on the phone."

"I told you he doesn't feel like talking."

"Malik, you better hurry up and put Isaiah on the phone, now," Michelle whispered through clenched teeth.

Malik covered the phone with his hand. He stood up and handed the phone to Isaiah. "Man, you'd better hurry up and answer this phone before she comes over here."

Isaiah snatched the phone away from Malik.

Isaiah covered the receiver with his hand. "I got this," Isaiah mimicked Malik sarcastically.

He reluctantly held the phone to his ear. "Hey Michelle, what's up? Sorry about dinner last night."

"What the hell is going on with you and Nicole? When the hell did she leave? And don't lie to me, Isaiah Jerome Mathis."

"She left last night, Michelle Denay Reed." He pulled the phone away from his ear, preparing for her outburst.

"She hasn't been home all night!! Where is she? What the hell did you do to Nicole, Isaiah?!"

"I didn't do shit to Nicole, Michelle. We had an argument, and she ran up outta here."

"And you just let her leave? What the hell were you two arguing about anyway? You two never fight. Where did she go? Why didn't she come over here? Why didn't she call me? Isaiah, if I found out you hurt my sister in any way, shape, or form, your black ass belongs to Grady Memorial Hospital. Oh, you got me cussing at work. Do I need to clock out and come over there? Hello?"

"Michelle, first of all, you need to relax. We had a small disagreement that got out of hand. I said some things I shouldn't have. She said some things she shouldn't have. I said some more things, she got mad and left," he lied.

"What the hell did you say? And more importantly, where could she have gone? We're the only family she has in Georgia. Maybe she has made it to the gallery by now. You need to check the gallery."

"That's a good idea," Isaiah responded.

"What about her friends, Marlon and Cynthia? Have they heard from her? Did you ask Pookie, my cousin, if she seen her? I know you better find her."

"I will. You call us if you hear from her."

"I promise, I will. I'm sorry for coming down on you like this, Isaiah. I know how much you love her. Please find her."

"I will. Here is your husband. Bye, Michelle."

"Bye, Isaiah." Isaiah handed the phone back to Malik.

"Hey, baby."

"Poo-Poo, I'm worried to death. Should I leave work and come help you guys?"

"No, baby, we can handle it. You try to have a good day at work. I love you."

"I love you too, please keep me posted." "I will."

"Bye, Poo-Poo."

"Bye, baby." Malik hung up the cordless phone. "So, what's the game plan, Dawg?"

"You get on the phone and call everyone you think she knows. She keeps her pink phone book in the top desk drawer on the left in the office upstairs. I'm going to take a quick shower and change, and then we can go to the gallery. What time do you have to be at work?"

"At two, but I can be late."

"What time is it now?" Isaiah asked. "Five after eleven."

"Give me five minutes, and we're out." Isaiah rushed upstairs and turned on the shower. He decided to call Nicole again.

Her voicemail answered.

He heard her sweet, soft voice over Mary J. Blige's '2U', then the voicemail beeped, and the recording began.

"I'm sorry."

# FIVE

Exactly thirty-seven minutes later, Brian knocked softly on Nicole's motel room door.

"Room Service," Brian spoke into the door.

Nicole felt better once the aspirin took effect, combined with a hot shower. She wrapped herself in the bed sheet with her blood-stained bra and matching panties underneath.

"Please come in. I apologize for the outfit; this is all I have."

His presence and warm, comforting smile immediately put her at ease. He was a large man, slightly overweight, though his height made it less obvious. His short, dark-brown hair perfectly accented his handsome, pudgy face. He had the brightest blue eyes she had ever seen. It was as if they were powered by lithium batteries.

He smiled softly as he entered the room. He wanted to hug her, but decided against it. He didn't want to frighten her.

She appeared to be so frail in her current condition. She could see the sorrow he felt for her in his eyes.

Brian walked in past her and placed the large bag of food on the small dining table. He loosened the cap on the bottled water before he handed it to her.

"Will you be dining alone, Madam?" Brian asked in his best British accent.

"No, please sit down." Nicole opened the heavy curtains as the brilliant fall sunshine lit up the room. She sat across from him as she removed the cap from the bottled water. She took a long, healthy swig. "I'm very thirsty."

"I see. You cleaned up well. See, I'm not scared." He smiled as he sat down.

"I am." She looked down at the table.

"You want to talk about it? I'm a great listener," he said as he unpacked the bag. "Here you go, I hope you like it."

He placed a large white styrofoam container in front of her.

"Thank you," she said. She opened the container as he handed her plastic cutlery. She inhaled the aroma as she said grace. She proceeded to eat. "This is delicious." She held the left side of her mouth as she chewed.

Brian could only assume that it hurt for her to chew.

"This is the best country cooking in Alabama." He began to eat.

She almost choked. "Alabama? Am I in Alabama? I thought I was still in Georgia."

"Don't worry, you're not far from home. Are you originally from Georgia?"

"No. I was born and raised in San Diego, California. I now reside in Atlanta."

"Oh, really, I have always wanted to go to California. I have seen California in movies and on TV. Is it really that beautiful?"

"It really is."

"So why would you leave California? If that's too personal, I understand."

"I wanted to start a new life."

"Did you move to Atlanta with your family?" he asked, making small talk.

Nicole shook her head no. She held down her head and shut her eyes. She took a deep breath and exhaled.

Brian decided to change the subject. "So, what do you do in Atlanta?"

"I am a part-time office manager and a portrait artist."

"Oh, really? I paint a little too. I don't consider myself an artist. It's more of a hobby. It helps me relax. Do you have a gallery?"

"We... I planned to open it next month."

Brian chose to put the focus on himself. "When I told you I was gay, you said you already knew. Is it obvious or something? Do I look gay? Please be honest."

She took another bite, chewed, and swallowed as Brian anxiously awaited a response.

She wiped the corners of her mouth and looked Brian directly in the eyes. "I knew because I'm gay, we know our own kind." She managed a weak smile. It had been years since she revealed her personal truth to a total stranger. It felt good to speak freely without the caution of being detected or judged.

Brian dropped his plastic fork into his container.

"I had no idea you were a lesbian. You mean another woman did this to you last night?" he said, referring to her beaten face and body. "She must have been a huge lesbian, or was it more than one?"

"I'm not a lesbian," she stated calmly as she continued eating.

"Ok, wait a minute, I don't understand. How can you be gay and not a lesbian? I don't understand."

"I was born male." She resumed eating.

"What? Are you serious?" Brian questioned. "I don't believe it. I have seen drag queens before, and you can always tell. No way!"

"I am not a drag queen. I am a transgender female, which means that I had a sex change, genital reassignment. I am now a complete functional woman."

Brian sat in absolute amazement as he gazed at the battered

Nicole. He ignored her bruises. "Look at you, your hands, your small shoulder, and arms, your height and weight. I can't imagine you ever being a man. You even have a woman's voice."

She felt slightly uncomfortable with him paying her such close attention. "I never had a masculine voice. I've always been feminine."

Brian sat back down at the table and shook his head in disbelief. He could only imagine what she looked like before the incident. "How long have you been a total woman?"

"Physically, I have been a transgender woman for over two years. Mentally, I've been a woman my whole life, even as a small child. At an early age, I knew that I was meant to be a girl. I vowed that when I grew up, if allowed, that I would make myself look the way I felt inside."

"Everything about you is so feminine that you must have looked like a girl when you were a boy."

"It would drive my parents crazy, especially my father. He didn't know what to do. He insisted that my mother should dress me in ultra-masculine clothes and cut my hair really close. That didn't help either. Other men in church would pull my father aside and say, 'If you aren't careful, brother Bennett, your daughter will grow up and be a dyke lesbian.' It would infuriate my father. 'That's my son,' He'd yell." Nicole laughed.

"So, how does he feel now?" Brian asked as her smile disappeared.

"I don't know, they threw me out at sixteen. My mother told me she didn't understand what I was going through, and she had to think of my little sister. I was never allowed to see my little sister again." Nicole lowered her eyes to the table.

"I'm sorry," Brian said, touching her hand. "I guess that's the reason I hide my sexuality. I would hate to lose my family. My parents don't know, or at least pretend they don't know. They don't bring it up, and neither do I. And you know what? I'm okay with that. I'm not a spokesperson for homosexuality. Being gay ain't my whole life, it's just a small piece of who I am. I don't feel that it is necessary to share my sexuality with people unless they want to know all of me. You understand?"

"I understand very well. For me, it was very... different. I suffered from gender dysphoria. It was never about sexuality. Now that I have obtained my true sexual identity, I don't feel that it is necessary to reveal the truth about my past."

Nicole's cell phone rang on the bed as they both stared at it.

Nicole stood up, looked at the caller ID, and recognized Michelle's work number. She assumed that Michelle had talked with Isaiah. She turned off her cell phone.

"If you need to answer that, I can..." Brian said.

"No, please let's finish eating." Nicole sat back down at the small dinette set.

"So, how did you take care of yourself when your parents threw you out? Did you stay with friends or other family members?"

"I had no friends growing up. All the neighborhood children would tease me and beat me up. As I got older, it became worse. My father never got involved. He said it was what I should expect from the lifestyle I had chosen. My father forbade his family from helping me, so I would be forced to come to my senses. I was turned away from the church because of my sexuality. Even youth shelters denied me. I was forced to take care of myself. Oftentimes, young transsexuals are forced to live on the streets because their parents or families disapprove of their chosen lifestyles. Older transsexuals adopt younger transsexuals as the older girls did for them. I began prostituting to survive, and that's when I met Peppa. She is an older transsexual from Chicago. I moved in with Peppa, and we became very close. To this day, I consider her to be my real mother. She made sure I completed high school. She has always believed in me and assisted me in making the right choices as far as doctors and hormonal therapy are concerned."

Nicole then realized that she needed to call Peppa. "Do you have any pictures of yourself before this happened to you?"

Nicole rose from the table and retrieved the matching wallet from her purse. She opened it and handed it to Brian.

He recognized the first picture in her wallet. "This must be your little sister. You two look exactly alike."

"Yes. She is my heart. Her name is Kyla, Kyla Nicole Bennett. She was nine years old in that picture," she stated proudly.

"She is absolutely adorable. How old is she now?"

"She is 24, her birthday is April 12."

"How does she feel about you now?"

"I haven't seen my sister in 15 years since my parents threw me out. She was my only true friend growing up; she loved me unconditionally."

"So, you two were very close?"

"Oh my gosh, we were like Siamese twins. She was all I had. I taught her everything — her letters and numbers, how to read and write. Her first words were my nickname, Jonnie." She smiled. "It was difficult in the beginning of our separation, and that's when Peppa started calling me Nicole. She explained that it would always remind me of her. I know I will see her again, and it's that very thought that keeps me going. I want her to be proud of me. I have often wondered what she will say or think about the new me. Or will she even remember me at all?"

"How could you ever forget a brother or sister? I'm an only child, and trust me, it has its benefits. But I can only imagine having someone, a sibling, to share my life with. Your sister probably thinks of you in the same way." He turned to the next set of photos of a young, sharply dressed man. "Who is this young man?"

"That is Isaiah's twelve-year-old son, Rashidi. He's a great kid."

"How did you two get along?"

"Excellent, he calls me his Atlanta mom."

Brian turned to the next set of pictures. He was mesmerized. "Oh my God, is this you? You look like a real woman; it's impossible to tell that you were ever anything else. You are so beautiful. You kind of remind me of Halle Berry with long hair. Is this your boyfriend in the picture with you?"

"He was my fiancé. His name is Isaiah."

Brian looked up from the wallet at Nicole. Even though she had been beaten up, he could envision her underlying beauty. He resumed looking at the pictures.

Both Nicole and Isaiah were standing in the picture. She stands approximately 5'8" and weighs 135 pounds, with long, naturally curly hair cascading over her right shoulder. Her hair is medium brown with light brown highlights. Her beauty is unreal, especially considering her past. Her huge, almond-shaped eyes flowed to her sleek, perfect nose. Her full, soft-looking lips are enhanced with a neutral shade of lipstick. Other than lipstick, it seemed she had on no makeup at all. Her creamy, light-brown complexion is blemish-free. Her supple smile brings out the apple in her cheeks.

"You were definitely meant to be a girl," he said without looking away from the picture.

Isaiah is equally as attractive as Nicole with his rich, deep-chocolate skin tone. He stood at least six feet two inches tall and one hundred ninety pounds, Brian guessed. Brian had never been attracted to African-American men before, but looking at a smiling Isaiah made him reconsider. Not only was Isaiah tall, but he was also solid with a great physique that only added to his rugged Adonis appeal. He had sexy, dark bedroom eyes and a strong black male nose. His precision-cut goatee and beard brought attention to his large, sensuous, brown lips. "He is gorgeous, you two look perfect together."

"He is the one who did this to me; he found out the truth about my past."

"Are you serious? How did he find out?" He looked up at her.

"Somehow, he found an old advertisement of me when I was a transsexual escort."

"No wonder you came in here like that last night, you poor thing," Brian said softly as he set the wallet down on the table. He stood up and hugged her.

"It's my fault, I should have told him the truth about me from the beginning."

"You can't beat yourself up about it. You did what you thought was best."

"What am I going to do? I lost everything," she cried into his shoulder.

# Six

Isaiah and Malik jumped into Isaiah's metallic, gray F-150 work truck. Isaiah backed out of the driveway, and they headed towards the gallery.

"I called the gallery on the house phone, and no one answered. Then, I spoke with Greg and Cynthia; they haven't heard from her. Denise and Nikki are at work."

Malik continued to look through Nicole's pink phone book. "Who is Peppa?"

"Nicole said she was like a mother to her while growing up in San Diego. Yeah, try her."

"Man, slow down, or neither one of us will have the chance to find Nicole." Malik dialed the number on his cell phone. "Do you know this woman?"

"I haven't met her in person, but I have talked to her a few times on the phone." He handed the phone to Isaiah.

The ringing phone awakened Peppa.

She looked at the caller ID. She recognized the area code as Atlanta.

She assumed that it was Nicole. "Hello, Nicole?"

"Good morning, Pepper," trying his best to speak proper

English. "This is Isaiah, Nicole's fiancé. How are you this morning?"

Peppa immediately sat up in her bed, suddenly attentive.

Clearing her throat, "I'm fine, how are you?" "I'm doing well, thank you for asking."

"I assumed you were Nicole calling from the gallery. I saw the Atlanta area code. They are installing the security system this morning, aren't they?"

"Yes, ma'am."

"Is she with you?"

"No ma'am, that's why I'm calling you. We are on the way to the gallery now, and I was wondering, have you heard from her? We had a little disagreement last night, and she took off."

"How long has she been gone?" Peppa inquired, trying not to sound alarmed.

"She left around seven-thirty last night."

"I haven't heard from her. I hope you two aren't arguing about anything serious."

"No ma'am, not really."

Peppa knew something was wrong. "Have you tried any of her friends? I know that she is very fond of a woman named Michelle. Have you tried her?"

"Yes, ma'am, I have."

"Does she still have the pink phone book?"

"Yes, ma'am, that is how we found your number. We have called all the numbers in her phone book; no one has heard from her or seen her. Do you have any more suggestions?"

"You know what, let me think about it and I will get back to you."

"And if you hear from her, please have her call me immediately."

"I sure will," Peppa said.

"Make sure to tell her that I'm sorry, and please call me. Thank you."

"You're welcome, and don't you worry. She'll be back before you know it. Goodbye, Isaiah."

"Bye."

Peppa hung up the phone and immediately began to worry. "I wonder if he knows? No, impossible, Nicole would have called me by now." Peppa rationalized.

She remembered the first time she met Nicole... She was casually strolling down the streets of Hillcrest, heading for the nightclubs, late one evening.

*She noticed a teenage child in a hideous, jet-black wig and men's clothing sitting at the bus stop. The child wore a bright shade of red lipstick and had a youthful, naturally pretty face. She could tell it was a boy by his clothing.*

*"Hi, pretty, how are you?" Peppa smiled at the child.*

*"Hi," he nervously replied.*

*"You okay, baby? You look lost. Are you from San Diego?"*

*"Yes, ma'am."*

*"So, what are you doing on the gay streets of Hillcrest so late at night? How old are you, sweetie?"*

*"I'm sixteen, I will be seventeen next month."*

*"Do you live in Hillcrest or somewhere close?"*

*"No, ma'am."*

*"Do you have a name, sweetheart?"*

*"I call myself Jonnie, my real name is Jonathan. Jonathan Bennett."*

*"Well, it's nice to meet you, Jonnie," Peppa said, extending her hand. "My name is Peppa."*

*They shook hands.*

*"Would you like to walk me to the club? It is only a few blocks up?"*

*"Okay." Jonnie stands up.*

*They started walking.*

*"You are so adorable. You remind me of myself when I was a child. Have you eaten?"*

"Yes, ma'am, I did." He smiled and looked away. "Stop calling me ma'am, my name is Peppa. My friends call me Peppa. So where do you live, Jonnie?"

"I have a hotel room downtown. A friend got it for me."

"You don't live with your family?"

"I don't want to talk about them. Please, if that's okay."

"It's okay. So how do you take care of yourself? Do you have a job?"

"I survive, ma'am," he replied, embarrassed.

"I heard that." Peppa smiled.

They stop on the corner in front of an adult novelty store.

"Let's go in here."

"They won't let me in there, I'm too young."

"If they stop us, I'll say you're my daughter." Peppa placed her arm around the child, and they walked into the store.

"I need to pick up some condoms and lubrication. Do you need some, Jonnie?" Jonnie shook his head, no.

"Of course, you do."

They walked past the clerk at the counter.

"Look at this."

They walked over to a display.

"Pick it up," Peppa instructed.

Jonnie picked up the gray plastic mirror on display. When he held it up to look at his reflection, the mirror whistled like a man when he spots an attractive female.

"That is really cute." Jonnie placed the mirror back on the display.

"I thought so too. Well, let's go get some condoms and get out of here." Peppa purchased an assortment of condoms and lubricant, and they left the store.

She handed a small bag of condoms and lubrication to Jonnie. "Make sure you use these each and every time you have sex, even oral sex. You understand?"

"Yes, ma'am...Peppa, I will. Thank you." Jonnie placed them in *his large, worn backpack that doubled as his purse.*

*They continued to walk down the street.*

*"So, why don't you live with your parents, Jonnie?" Jonnie looked away.*

*"My parents hate me because I want to be a woman."*

*"Do you have any brothers or sisters?"*

*Tears welled in the corners of his eyes, and his bottom lip began to quiver.*

*"Honey, you don't have to talk about it. I'm sorry for putting you on the spot like that."*

*"I have a little sister; her name is Kyla Nicole Bennett. She is the only person who loves me, and they took her away from me," he cried.*

*"It's gonna be okay," Peppa consoled. "She has a beautiful name. You really miss her, huh? How old is she?"*

*"She's nine years old in the picture I have. She turned ten in April." Jonnie reached into his backpack and removed his only picture of his sister. He handed it to Peppa.*

*"She is so beautiful, you two look exactly alike. Are you twins?" Jonnie shook his head no.*

*Peppa handed back the wallet-sized picture. "You know the same thing happened to me when I was your age. My parents threw me out of their house."*

*He looked up at Peppa.*

*"How long have you been on the streets?"*

*"Just a few days, I guess." He wiped away the tears. "I went downtown, and this man offered me twenty dollars to... and I did it. Then another guy approached me, and I did it again. At the end of the night, I had over a hundred dollars. They think I'm a girl."*

*"Is that what you want to be, a girl?"*

*"Yes, more than anything in the whole world. I want to be a woman. Does that sound silly?"*

*"Of course not," Peppa smiled.*

*"I want to be just like you."*

"Well, guess what, I started out just like you. And if I can look like this, so can you."

"Are you serious? You were a boy?" Jonnie asked in amazement.

"Yes, ma'am," Peppa responded, acknowledging the female inside Jonnie. "I've had my face reconstructed and my nose done twice. I've had a chin implant, and that's just my face."

"Well, you're certainly a beautiful woman today."

"Well, thank you, Jonnie. You will become a beautiful woman too, if that's what you really want."

"How did you get your breasts?" he asked in admiration.

"These are implants, but you need to start at the beginning with female hormones."

"Hormones?"

"There is medicine for people like us who want to change sexes. You can either inject them or take them orally."

"Really, and they will give me breasts?" he questioned enthusiastically.

Peppa laughed because she found Jonnie's naivety endearing.

"Not only will hormones give you breasts, but they will make your physical appearance much softer. Your hair and nails will also grow. And because you are so young, they will really have an impact on your feminine development."

"That's awesome. Where can I get some hormones?"

"I could give you some, but it would be best to find yourself a doctor to prescribe you your own." Peppa stopped. "Well, here's the club that I'm going to tonight. Thank you for hanging out with me, Jonnie." She reached into her purse and handed Jonnie her business card. "This is my business card; it has my phone number on it. What are you doing tomorrow?"

"Nothing."

"Call me tomorrow and maybe you can come over to my house, if you're not too busy," Peppa smiled.

"I won't be busy. What time tomorrow?"

*"How about noon? I will give you directions to my apartment, okay?"*

*"Thank you, Peppa." Jonnie instinctively hugged her. "Have fun in there."*

*"I will. You be careful and don't forget to call me. You promise?"*

*"I promise. Bye." Jonnie turned around and started to walk away.*

*"Jonnie, wait," Peppa walked back up to Jonnie.*

*"Yes," Peppa reached inside her purse and handed the gray plastic whistling mirror to Jonnie.*

*"Here's a little present for you, pretty," Peppa said.*

*Jonnie hugged Peppa again. "Thank you, Peppa."*

*"You're welcome, sweetheart. See you tomorrow."*

Peppa, smiling, sat up against the backboard of her immense, California-King-sized bed. "I might as well get up." She said aloud as she found her cable remote and turned on her flat screen television. She pulled the covers off her legs.

**"Both bodies have been identified in last night's car accident on Interstate 805," said the morning news anchor. "It appears to be the result of drunk driving. The first driver has been identified as 42-year-old Paul Granger, previously convicted of drunk driving in 1997. The second driver has been identified as a 24-year-old San Diego State Graduate, Kyla Nicole Bennett."**

Peppa froze in horror.

# Seven

"I know I don't know you that well, but is it really that bad? There's no hope at all?"

Nicole looked up at Brian. "He was trying to kill me."

"So how did it happen? Where did he get your old advertisement?" Brian released her.

"I don't know," she recalled. "We always have Sunday dinner with his best friend's family. So, we were going to their house this week. I was already dressed with my purse and keys waiting by the front door. All I had to do was put on my lipstick and heels. Isaiah is a mechanic and was at his shop trying to meet the deadlines he set for his customers. That's when I heard his tires screech in the front driveway. He parked his truck next to my car. I figured he was in a hurry, so I hurried downstairs to meet him at the door. He shoved the front door open and just stood there glaring at me. It was as though he had never seen me before. He was breathing so hard through his nostrils. You could see his heartbeat thumping in his neck. I have never seen him so upset."

Instantaneously, Nicole was transported back to standing before Isaiah.

"Isaiah, are you okay?" she asked. "Baby, what happened?" She reached out to touch him, and he pushed her hands away.

He threw the manila envelope at her, and it hit her in the chest and fell to the floor.

"What is this? What's wrong?" she pleaded as she bent down and retrieved the manila envelope.

"Open it."

"What is this?" She fumbled with the envelope and peered inside. She read the heading of the familiar publication as she let it fall from her hands onto the tiled entryway.

Nicole was stunned. She felt as if someone was holding a loaded gun to her head. She was paralyzed with fear. She wanted to run but couldn't move.

Isaiah, without a doubt, now knew the truth.

"Fuck this shit, are you a fucking man?" He felt the tears forming in the corners of his eyes as his anger grew.

Nicole didn't know what to say; she was at a loss for words.

"I asked you a question, are you a fuckin' man?"

Unconsciously, Nicole took a step backwards. She stood there helplessly.

Isaiah turned around and engaged both locks on the front door. "ARE YOU A FUCKIN' MAN!?!" he erupted at the top of his lungs.

"No. Why would you ask me that?"

"That magazine says that you're a passable transsexual and you're telling me to my face that you ain't a man?"

"Isaiah, please, do I look like a man?" Tears began to fall from her eyes. "Do I act like a man? When you make love to me, does it feel like you're fucking a man? Maybe that's a question you need to ask yourself."

She saw the first blow coming and tried to duck as she screamed his name. "ISAIAH!?!"

He struck her hard in her mouth with his massive fist.

She stumbled back from the impact as she screamed loudly from *the pain. "ISAIAH, PLEASE!?!" She tried to shield her face. "SOMEBODY, PLEASE HELP ME!?!"*

*He delivered another crushing blow to her left eye and another to her right eye.*

*"HELP ME, PLEASE, SOMEBODY HELP ME!?!"*

*She reached out with her nails and dug into the flesh of his face and neck.*

*He grabbed hold of the top of her dress and ripped it down the center. He struck her repeatedly.*

*She saw her life flash before her eyes.*

*He slapped her with the back of his hand, which sent her reeling to the floor, halfway on the carpet of the living room.*

*She was on her back, vulnerable and exposed, as he straddled her. She could see the tears flowing from his eyes.*

*He reached down and forcefully removed the ring he once placed so lovingly on the same finger. He threw it across the living room and prepared to end her life. He closed his tear-stained eyes and reached for her throat. His intentions were obvious.*

*She knew what was coming next. "ISAIAH, PLEASE, DON'T DO THIS, I LOVE YOU!" She prevented his hand from reaching her throat with her own flailing fists.*

*He leaned forward and gripped her throat.*

*She took both of her strong thumb nails and dug into Isaiah's eye sockets. He yelled out in agonizing pain as he released his grip on her throat.*

*She then kneed him squarely in his groin as he collapsed to her right side, holding his testicles. She quickly scrambled to her feet, unlocked the front door, grabbed her purse and keys, and ran to her car.*

"And that is how I got away."

Brian's mouth was agape, enthralled with her vivid reenactment. "Unbelievable," he responded softly.

"I feel the whole situation is entirely my fault. If I had told him the truth in the beginning, none of this would have happened," Nicole rationalized.

"You can't blame yourself. That won't change a thing. If you had told Isaiah the truth in the beginning, your relationship might never have happened. The only way you both will resolve this issue is by talking to each other. "Have you talked to him since you left?"

"He's left messages."

"That means he's ready to talk. See if he has left you any new ones."

She retrieved her cell phone and turned it on.

Once the cell phone powered up, it indicated that she had received new messages.

She held the cell phone to her ear after she pressed the listen to messages button.

Brian began to clean off the small table.

"You have three new messages and three saved messages," the phone chirped cheerily.

"New message, Hello, Mrs. Mathis, My name is Simon Felding with Swift Security Systems. We had a ten o'clock installation this morning. Hopefully, you are enroute. If not, I can only wait for five more minutes. Please feel free to reschedule an installation appointment, and thank you for your business."

She pressed 9.

"Message saved, new message."

"Hi Sweetie, how are you feeling? I just talked with Isaiah, and he told me everything." Michelle said.

Nicole's heartbeat accelerated.

"Girl, I cussed that asshole out and threatened him with Grady Hospital. Where are you? We're worried to death; he and Malik went to the gallery looking for you."

Nicole smiled at Brian, "This is my best friend, and they are looking for me."

Brian smiled back.

"See there, what did I tell you?" Brian whispered.

She resumed listening to the messages.

"They are calling all over Atlanta looking for you. Where are you? Girl, I can't concentrate on my job worrying about you. At least let me know that you're okay. Tell me something so I can let Isaiah off the hook before he hurts himself. Call me Sis, I love you. Now bring your ass home. Bye."

She hugged Brian.

"You were right, Brian." She smiled.

She felt as though she had known Brian for years, like a best friend she had been reacquainted with.

She pressed 9.

"Message saved. New message."

"I'm sorry."

"Listen, Brian."

She pressed 1.

Brian heard the short message.

"Now, it's time for you to call him. Go ahead and dial his number."

"Brian, I can't."

"Here," he took the phone from Nicole. "I will call him then. What's the number?"

"Brian, I don't think…"

"What are you going to do, stay in this crummy motel forever? Trust me, Nicole, what's the number?"

"770-555-5368."

He dialed the numbers.

"It's ringing. Here, take the phone." He handed the cell phone back to Nicole.

She placed it to her ear.

After the third ring, the automatic voicemail answered.

"Hello, this is Nicole…What up, this is Isaiah." Nicole's voice continued on the message. "Sorry, we are unavailable to take your call at this time," Isaiah's voice concluded the message. "You know what to do, leave a message...beep."

She ended the call.

"He's not answering the home phone. Maybe he sees it's me calling and had a change of heart."

"Well, call your best friend. Maybe she knows where he is."

She dialed Michelle's work number.

"Hello, this is Michelle Reed; may I help you, please?"

"Hi, Michelle, it's me, Nicole."

"Hey, Sister, hold on, let me close my door... Girl, what the hell is going on? We are going crazy looking for you. Where the hell are you at?"

"I'm near Birmingham."

"Birmingham! As in Birmingham, Alabama? What the hell are you doing in Birmingham? Nicole, what the hell is going on? It's not like you, not to talk to me."

"Nothing is going on, I promise," she lied.

"Nicole, are you okay? I can meet you in Birmingham."

"Michelle, I am fine. I will be home before you know it. How is Isaiah? I tried calling him at home, and no one answered."

"Isaiah and Malik went to the gallery, trying to find you. They found your pink phone book, and they are calling everyone you know."

Nicole became alarmed. *What if they called Peppa and told her what happened? She would be on her way to Atlanta with her nine-millimeter.*

"Isaiah is going crazy. Make sure you call him on his cell phone."

"I don't remember his new cell phone number."

"Girl, hold on, it's in my phone. As a matter of fact, just call Malik's cell; they are together. And call him right now, before he kills himself and my husband. And call me right back when you are finished talking with them. You promise?"

"I will, I promise, Michelle. Love you."

"Love you, too." Nicole ended the call and stared blankly at her cell phone.

"Well, what are you waiting for?" Brian overheard the conversation.

"I'm trying to build up the nerve."

"Call him already."

Nicole was dialing Malik's cell number on her cell phone when her phone started ringing with an incoming call.

"Who is it?" Brian asked.

"It's Peppa," Nicole responded. "Hello?" Nicole answered. "I was just about to call you Momma, after I talked to Isaiah... Hello, Peppa? Are you there?"

"Nicole?"

"Hey, Momma, I can barely hear you. Hello? Did Isaiah call you? I don't know what Isaiah told you, but..."

"Are you driving? Are you alone, or is someone with you?"

"Are you feeling okay, Peppa? Isaiah found out the truth about me and..."

"What I have to tell you doesn't concern Isaiah. Are you driving?"

"No, Momma, what?"

"Are you alone?"

"No, Momma, why? You're starting to scare me. What happened?"

"I...I don't know how to tell you this," Peppa stammered.

"Whatever it is, it's okay. Just say it, please."

"It's about your sister. Kyla is dead."

# Eight

"What now?" Malik asked.

"Call the house phone, maybe she tried to call there."

Malik dialed Isaiah's home number on his cell phone.

"Before the message ends, enter the code 132#," Isaiah instructed.

Malik entered the code.

"Nothing, no messages." Malik reported.

Isaiah's cell phone rang. Isaiah reached into the armrest to retrieve his phone.

"I'll get it, you concentrate on the road." Malik picked up Isaiah's cell phone.

"It could be Nicole."

Malik read the caller ID. "It's Michelle."

"Maybe she's heard from Nicole."

"Hey, baby, what's up? Why are you calling on Isaiah's phone?" Malik answered.

"I told Nicole to call you guys on your phone. I thought Isaiah and Nicole would still be talking on your phone." Michelle answered.

"So, you heard from her?" Malik asked.

"She talked to Nicole?" Isaiah eagerly questioned.

"Yes, she talked to Nicole. Now, will you just chill the fuck out?"

"Put her on speakerphone." Malik pressed the button.

"Hello, Michelle, did you talk to Nicole?" Isaiah asked aloud.

"Yes, didn't she call you guys? She said as soon as she hung up with me, she would call you on Malik's phone. What the hell is she doing in Birmingham, Alabama?"

"Alabama?" they both said in unison.

"That's what she told me, near Birmingham, Alabama. She said she was fine, that she would be home in no time."

Isaiah turned left and headed for the interstate. "You down?" he asked Malik.

"Let's roll."

"Hey Michelle, did she say exactly where she was in Alabama?" Isaiah asked.

"No, I asked if she wanted me to meet her in Birmingham, she said no."

"Let us hang up and call her to find out exactly where the hell she is." Isaiah suggested.

"Go ahead and call me right back." Michelle agreed.

"I will." Malik hung up the phone.

"What the hell is she doing in Alabama?" Malik asked Isaiah.

Malik dialed Nicole's cell with Isaiah's phone.

"I have no idea." Malik pushed the speakerphone button on the touchscreen.

The phone continued to ring, unanswered, and then the voicemail picked up.

"Hello, this is Nicole. Sorry, I'm unavailable to answer your call. Please be kind and leave your name, number, and a brief message, and I promise I will get back to you at my earliest opportunity. Thank you for calling, and may God bless you in every way possible."

"Hey, baby... I mean, I am so sorry for all the pain that I caused you. I promise that it will never happen again. We really need to talk. I'm on the way to Birmingham, and I have no idea where you are. Please, call me right now so I can get to you."

Malik interrupted. "What up, Nicole? It's your boy, Malik. Please help us get to you. You need to call us right now."

"We all need you in our lives," Isaiah interjected. "Man, hang up the phone." Malik hung up the phone.

"I said that so she will tell us where she is," Isaiah explained to Malik.

# NINE

Peppa's phone rang.

"Hello," she answered quickly.

"Hi Peppa, it's Brian again. Sorry it took me so long to get back to you. We had a lot to do."

"How is Nicole?"

"She's really upset, but she's hanging in there. Do you have a pen and paper handy?"

"Yes, please go ahead."

"Her flight is Delta 172. She will arrive at the San Diego Airport this afternoon at 4:54 P.M., California time. She said please make sure that you're there to pick her up."

"Of course, I will be there."

"Isaiah just left; he came to pick up her car. He was terribly upset that he didn't get to see Nicole before she left."

"Yes, I talked with Isaiah earlier. I gave him my address. He said he would try to be here for her. He didn't even know she had a sister."

"He didn't know a lot of things about Nicole," Brian interjected. "I have a favor to ask of you, Peppa. Please take care of her."

"You know I will, Brian. I can't tell you how much I appreciate the loving kindness you have shown my baby. Thank you so much for being there for her. God truly works in mysterious ways."

"You know we instantly connected from the moment we first laid eyes on one another. Please let me know when she arrives there. Tell her that I love her."

"I will."

"Goodbye, Peppa."

"Goodbye, Brian, and I will definitely keep in touch."

"Thank you. Goodbye."

# TEN

Isaiah and Malik returned to Isaiah's home at 4:47 P.M.

Malik fell onto the couch, and Isaiah stretched out on his back on the plush carpeting in the living room, laying his keys, baseball cap, and sunglasses next to him.

"Damn, I'm tired." Malik stretched out and yawned.

"Hey man, thanks for taking the day off. Good looking out."

"You know you, my nigga." Malik smiled.

"You know, driving back to Atlanta alone gave me a chance to think. I thought about all the lies she told me, her parents, and the car accident. Her niece in the picture in the office is actually her little sister. And on top of all that, she's a man. What else did she lie to me about? Man, to be honest, I don't give a fuck if I ever see her again."

"I totally feel you, man, but I think you're forgetting what she helped you accomplish."

"Any good woman could have done that."

"Any good woman didn't do it; Nicole did. She stuck by your ass and believed in you from day one. She put off her own dreams to help you accomplish yours."

Isaiah sat up. "And what's that supposed to mean? I should turn into a faggot and marry it?"

"I'm not saying that you should still have sexual feelings for her, but you owe her. You know, I had a chance to think, as well, and I honestly put myself in your shoes. Nicole has never been a man to you, to me, or to anybody else we know. And if it weren't for that dumb ass magazine, we would have never known. All I'm saying is that you need to take a little time and reconsider all your options."

"Ain't no options, she's a he or least was born a he. Look at how this shit is unraveling. Why haven't I talked to her since she left? It must be a sign that it's not meant to be."

"It's a sign, alright, a sign for you to take your black ass upstairs and get some sleep, you trippin.' You know I love you, right?"

"Man, you trippin' now."

"Hold up. Hear me out. We grew up together since elementary school in Florida, right?"

"And?"

"And what I'm trying to say is there ain't nobody on this earth, except God, that knows you as I do. I'm saying, just think about it."

"She's a fuckin' man, Malik. And now I know it."

Malik stood up and squatted in front of Isaiah. "I can remember the first time you met Nicole. You called me all excited and shit, sounding like a teenage boy. You said you just had lunch with the most beautiful, intelligent, and classiest woman you had ever met. And the more time you spent with her, the more you felt her. Now, think about the first time she let you hit it. You called me at two o'clock in the morning, talking shit about how you think you love her. You said she was perfect, and no other woman mattered anymore; she changed you. I remember the first time I met Nicole. Man, you were so fucking proud when you introduced her to me. It wasn't the way she looked to me, but it was the way she looked at you, that let me know she was

Mrs. Mathis. I am aware that major shit has changed between the two of you. I'm not saying she is worthy to be Mrs. Mathis now. But she is a friend if nothing else, and you need to be there for her."

"Dawg, you trippin'," Isaiah replied.

"No, I'm right. Now take your ass upstairs and get some rest. You have a lot of shit to do—put someone in charge at the garages, book flights, and a hotel room. You already have Peppa's address. I'm headed home. Call me tomorrow." He stood up and reached into his pocket for his keys.

The front door opened, and in walked Michelle.

"Knock, knock," Michelle said. "Where's Nicole?"

She closed the door behind herself and started to walk up the stairs. "Nicole," she yelled upstairs.

Malik intercepted his wife so she couldn't get a good look at Isaiah. "Hey, baby," he kissed her passionately on the mouth.

Isaiah quickly stood up and put his sunglasses and baseball cap back on. "How was work?"

"It was work. Where's my girl? I see her car in the driveway. I haven't heard from her all day." She looked over her husband's shoulder at Isaiah.

"Isaiah and I just got back from Alabama. We had to go get her car. She had to rush to California."

"California!" She pulled away from her husband and glared at Isaiah.

"Yeah, she rushed to San Diego, her sister died," Malik said.

"Okay, so let me get this straight. She's in San Diego, California, because her sister died, right?"

Malik and Isaiah both shook their heads yes in unison.

"Is it her older or younger sister?"

"Her baby sister," Isaiah answered.

"Y'all can do better than that. She doesn't even have a sister. I talked to her this morning she told me she was in Alabama. Now, she's in California, right?"

"Baby, he's telling the truth, that little girl's picture in the office is her little sister," Her husband interjected.

"She told me that was her niece, Kyla Nicole. They have the same name because they look so much alike. How did she supposedly die?" She looked at both of them skeptically, back and forth.

"A car accident, a drunk driver hit her, killed her instantly," Isaiah added.

"How did you find out? You finally talked to her?" She stared at both of them suspiciously.

"Peppa called Malik's cell phone after she told Nicole what happened. She said Brian was sending Nicole to California."

"Who the hell is Brian? Y'all know what? Y'all better quit playing with me." Michelle kicked off her low-heeled pumps. "Where is Nicole?" She removed her small hoop earrings. Then she pulled her hair back into a ponytail with a ponytail holder worn on her wrist.

"We telling the truth, Poo-Poo." He tried to hug his wife.

"Don't 'Poo-Poo' me." She pushed him away.

Malik removed his cell phone from his pocket. "Here. Her number should still be in my cell. Here it is. You call her. Her name is Peppa."

"I know who Peppa is." She snatched the phone away from her husband. She pressed the dial button.

"She better be there or we all going to Grady tonight."

"Michelle, calm down." She gave her husband the middle finger.

"And why did you put on a cap and sunglasses in the house?" she asked Isaiah. "Ain't nobody answering!"

"Then leave a message," Isaiah snapped.

"Hello, Peppa, this is Michelle. I have talked with you several times on the phone. How are you doing? I just got out of work, and I have been worried all day about my best friend. Now, I really need to talk with her. I sincerely pray that she is there with you, or

I am about to go to a maximum-security penitentiary, in solitary confinement for double homicide."

"Hello?" Peppa answered.

"Hello, is this Peppa?"

"Hi, Michelle, how are you?"

"I'm worried to death. Is Nicole there with you, ma'am?"

"Not yet, but she's on the way. Were you informed that her sister died? She was killed by a drunk driver."

"Will you please have her call me as soon as she arrives, please?"

"I sure will as soon as I get her settled in."

"Yes, ma'am. Tell her that I miss her and love her very much. And thank God you picked up the phone. You just saved three lives."

"Okay. I will have her call as soon as she can. And tell Isaiah that the nearest hotel to me is the Hillcrest Suites on University. Goodbye."

"Goodbye, ma'am." She handed the phone back to her husband. "I'm sorry that I doubted you." She kissed him on the mouth.

She then whipped around to face Isaiah. "So, what happened between you and Nicole? Why did she leave in the first place? I see those scratches on your face and neck."

"Baby, it's a long story, and we're both tired as hell. Can we talk about this when we get home?" Malik intervened.

"She is my best friend, and I have a right to know. Remember what I said about Grady, Isaiah?"

"Michelle, Nicole really needs Isaiah there with her. We need to let this man get some sleep. He has a lot of business to handle before he can leave. You need to think of Nicole right now. I promise I will tell you everything, once we get home, okay?"

"Okay, Poo-Poo," she kissed him lightly on the lips.

Then she spun around to face Isaiah. "You better hurry up and get your tired ass to bed so you can get your sorry ass to San Diego. And you better not come back unless Nicole is with you."

Michelle hugged Isaiah. "Please bring her back." She kissed him on the cheek. "Give her that from me and tell her that I love her."

"I will."

Malik escorted his wife to the front door. "Keep your head up, Dawg. If you need me, you know what to do."

"Thanks for everything, man."

They hugged and shook hands simultaneously.

"Call me tomorrow."

"I will, man."

"Goodnight, Isaiah."

"Goodnight, Michelle."

# ELEVEN

"Girl, she won't talk, she won't eat. What the hell am I supposed to do? She's been like this for five days." Peppa explained.

"When is the funeral?" Peppa's best friend, Candace, asked.

"Tomorrow morning, at eleven," Peppa answered. "Is Nicole going to attend the funeral?"

"I don't know, that's the only thing she's said in the last five days. Is the funeral today?"

"How does her face and body look? Did the bruises and the swelling heal?"

"They are fading rapidly. Nothing a little makeup can't cover up. Thank goodness her mother is a licensed cosmetologist. Trust me, if I can get her out of that bed, she will be sickening (beautiful) at the funeral."

"Are you going to the funeral with her tomorrow?"

"Hell no. I don't even deal with my own family, why would I deal with hers?"

"How long has it been since she's last seen her family?"

"Since she was sixteen years old."

"That is so sad what they did to that poor girl, took her sister away from her. Have you heard from her ex-fiancé, Isaiah, today?"

"Girl, he came by twice yesterday. I thought he would never leave. Miss Candace, girl, I crept up to the front door and looked out through the peephole. That man is sickening (beautiful) down (completely)!"

"What did you say to him?"

"Nothing, I didn't even answer the door. I thought he was going to kick it in. He keeps calling here. I already cussed his ass out for beating my daughter the way he did. You saw her face when she first got here. I told her more than once that he wants to talk with her, and it's like she doesn't hear me. He acts like he really cares for her. Hopefully, she will come to her senses soon. I don't know how long I can be a prisoner in my own home."

"So why did you give him your number and address?"

"He already had my number; he got it from her phonebook. And when I gave him my address, I had no idea that he tried to kill her."

"See Miss Peppa, that is why I always tell the trade (men) what I am, up front. That way, there are no surprises."

"Girl, it's obvious what you are up front. Looking like Mike Tyson with a wig on, talking about what you tell the trade up front. You dragon queens sure do kill me." Peppa laughed.

"Fuck you, you bald-headed bitch."

"I'm sorry, Miss Candace, but you know I keeps it real bitch."

"Whatever."

"I feel so sorry for that poor child. She's lost so much, I'm afraid this might break her." Peppa heard the toilet flush.

"Nicole, are you okay?" Peppa yelled down the hall. "Hold on, Miss Candace."

Peppa set the receiver down and walked down the hallway to the guest bathroom. She discreetly pushed open the bathroom door.

Nicole was standing in front of the bathroom mirror in one of

Peppa's flannel nightgowns, examining her body. Nicole saw Peppa and gave her a big hug.

"I love you, mama," Nicole said, kissing her on the cheek.

"I love you more," she kissed Nicole back on the forehead. Nicole looked at her reflection again.

"I look a mess," she pouted.

"You are still a raving beauty. You just remain thankful that man didn't kill you."

"But he did kill me, he ruined my life."

"You have to keep in mind that you played a role in that as well. You know I have always kept it real with you, and that I love you very much. I told you from the very beginning that this life that we live wasn't going to be easy, especially for you. You are a part of a rare group of unclockable (undetectable), post-op transsexuals. Not only are you beautiful inside and out, but you are also gifted. Everything you are going through is for a reason. What that reason is, I don't know. But I do know that I love you." She stroked Nicole's bushy, shoulder-length tresses.

Nicole looked Peppa straight in the eyes. "I want to die."

"Please don't say that. I understand that you're in a lot of pain right now. Keep in mind that the sun will shine again. It is always darkest before dawn. God didn't carry you through thirty-one years of life to let you go now."

"So why is God doing this to me?" she asked.

"It is not what God is doing to us; it is what God allows us to do to ourselves. Life is all about choices, whether they are good or bad, and the lives we live are based on the choices we have made."

"Why did she have to die? There is so much I wanted to share with her."

"Maybe God thought it was time for her to come home. You never know. Maybe God will allow her to see you at the funeral. Are you even strong enough to attend her funeral?"

"I have to be there for my baby sister, Yammy."

"Yammy? That must have been her nickname?"

"Yes, she loved sweet potatoes as a baby."

"Well, I won't let you pay your last respects to Yammy looking like this." Peppa smiled as they both looked into the mirror. "By the time I get done with you, they will think you are a supermodel." Peppa loosely piled Nicole's unruly hair on the top of her head. "You know Isaiah is here?" she said nonchalantly.

Nicole spun around to face Peppa. "Here, like in San Diego, here?"

"Yes, ma'am." Peppa smiled.

"How long has he been here? Where is he at? What did he say?" Nicole questioned frantically.

She held Nicole's face in both hands. "Slow down. He arrived yesterday, and he's been here twice. He's been calling all day."

"What did he say? Does he want to get back together? What did he say?"

"I don't know because I cussed him out the first time he called. I haven't answered the phone or front door since. What was I supposed to tell him?"

The phone in her bedroom audibly signaled that it was off the hook.

"I forgot I had Miss Candace on the phone."

"I remember Miss Candace. How is she doing?"

"She's still a brick (unattractive). Let me go hang it up." Peppa walked down the hall back to her bedroom.

Nicole turned off the bathroom light and followed Peppa into her bedroom.

"Your home is still beautiful. You completely changed everything. I love this," pointing to an enormous 100-gallon aquarium in the corner of her huge bedroom. "I can't believe you still have this."

It was an 18" x 24" immaculately framed portrait Nicole drew of Peppa when Nicole was a teenager.

"Of course, I have it. Where else would it be? The guest

bedroom you're in is filled with your art, old and new. You didn't even notice. I bet you don't remember these."

She reached into one of her drawers and handed Nicole a large pink photo album.

Nicole sat on the edge of Peppa's gigantic, California king-sized bed. She opened the photo album.

"Oh my gosh, I was hideous." Nicole and Peppa laughed as they looked at pictures of Nicole early in her transition. "What did you do, save every ugly picture of me that I ever took?"

"What do you mean by ugly? You have always been beautiful to me, except right there."

They laughed.

"I have pictures of every stage of your transformation. Turn to the back; I bet you don't remember these. That was the day you left California, I cried like a baby."

"So did I."

"Did I ever tell you how proud I am of you? You're a lot stronger than you give yourself credit for. With all the trials and tribulations that you have faced, you continue to grow. My daughter, the artist, is soon to be in her own gallery. I have always told that you were a great artist."

"Thank you, mama, I owe it all to you. Since the day you found me, you have always believed in and supported me in every choice I have ever made. You always told me that life is what I make it, and you were right. I should have listened to you. I should have told Isaiah everything about my past before we became serious."

"Don't blame yourself, child. Whether you told him or not, he knows now. And if you were meant to be, you will be. If not, life goes on. Now give me back my photo album, we have lots of work to do."

# Twelve

Knock...knock...knock... at the front door.

Peppa gave herself the once-over in the ornate, full-length mirror that was mounted in the foyer. She had put on her good hair and spent extra time on her makeup in order to impress Isaiah.

She took a deep breath and opened the front door. "Please come in," she said courteously to Isaiah.

Peppa could sense that he was uncomfortable.

He immediately recognized the elegant, comfortable style in which Nicole decorated their home. "Thank you. Nicole said she got her taste from you. I believe her now. This is really nice."

"Thank you, Isaiah. Let's have a seat in the living room, it's straight ahead. Can I offer you something to drink?"

"Uh, no, thank you. Is Nicole here? May I see her, please?"

"There are a few things we need to discuss first. Beginning with what you did or attempted to do to my baby."

"You know what, I will take that drink. Do you have any Brandy or Hennessy?"

"Straight or on the rocks?"

"I'll take the first one straight, please."

"Coming right up, please have a seat." She went into the kitchen.

Isaiah sat on the edge of the black leather couch.

"Nicole decorates similarly to you. You did decorate yourself, didn't you?"

"Yes, I did. I think it's comfortable." She spoke loudly from the kitchen.

"Nicole told me that you were like her mother growing up, that she's known you since she was sixteen."

"Yes, I remember it like it was yesterday. I met her about ten blocks from here. She was scared and shy, but she instantly opened up to me. From the moment I laid eyes on her, I knew we were going to be close."

She casually sauntered into the living room carrying their drinks. She extended his drink to him and immediately pulled it back.

"Do you promise to behave like a gentleman at all times, during and after our conversation?"

"I promise."

"No matter what we discuss, you will not become violent in any way, shape, or form?"

"No, ma'am, I promise." He said as he rubbed his hands down his pants leg.

"And you will not attempt to force yourself upon me if I become intoxicated?" Peppa asked with a straight face.

"No, ma'am." Isaiah blinked rapidly.

"Damn, you said that kind of fast. Here you go." She handed the drink to Isaiah.

"Thank you."

"You are welcome." She slid him a marble coaster to place his drink on the black marble and glass coffee table. Peppa sat adjacent to Isaiah on the matching love seat.

Isaiah could faintly distinguish that Peppa was born male now that he was looking directly at her.

It may have been the obvious wig or her voice. She wore an elegant, floor-length black satin, two-piece lingerie ensemble with black, open-toed, feather-trimmed mules.

"Nicole reminded me a great deal of myself at that age, except I wasn't naturally that pretty. She brought a ray of sunshine to my life, and you nearly took that away from me."

Isaiah swallowed his drink in one gulp.

"Please don't get me wrong, I don't completely blame you. This has happened before. Can I get you another drink?"

"Yes, please."

Peppa stood up from the loveseat. "Straight or on the rocks?"

"On the rocks, thank you."

She headed for the kitchen. Isaiah noticed that Peppa was somewhat attractive for an older he-she.

She definitely looked like a woman from the back, Isaiah determined. She was short, slightly overweight, with a big butt.

Ray-Ray, a mechanic at one of his shops, would love her, he thought.

"Is Nicole asleep?"

"No, she asked me to talk to you first." She walked back into the living room. "Here you go." She handed the drink to him.

"Thank you." He took a sip. "Too strong? I have more Coke."

"No, it's fine." Isaiah placed his drink onto the coffee table as Peppa resumed her place on the loveseat.

"So, Isaiah, how do you honestly feel about Nicole? Now that everything is in the open." Peppa picked up her drink from the coffee table.

"I care a great deal about Nicole. That's why I'm here. I want to be here for her if she needs me, because I know that she would be there for me."

"What about your upcoming nuptials?"

"I'm sure we won't be married."

"That is perfectly understandable." She took a sip. "Now, what if you had met Nicole and she told you that she was transgendered from the beginning? Would you have continued to date her?"

Isaiah picked up his drink and took a long, healthy swig. "That's hard to say," he replied, trying to recollect their initial meeting.

"The first time I saw her, she was pumping gas at a gas station. I think she was driving a white Mitsubishi Galant, yes. She was wearing pink shorts and a little white tank top, with pink sandals. I was on my way to lunch, and she looked up and smiled at me. She was so mutha-fuckin' fine. Excuse my language."

"No need to apologize, we're both adults. Please continue." She took another sip from her highball glass.

"Her hair was hanging over one shoulder. I managed to get my car through two lanes of traffic and pulled up next to her. She had the prettiest smile I had ever seen. And if she had told me she was born a man or a trans-whatever, I would have had to say no."

"The correct terminology is post-op transsexual or transgendered. And this is exactly the reason why she didn't tell you. And that is not an excuse; it's the truth. It's like a former crack-head or alcoholic changes their life, and the first person they meet, they tell them about their former addiction or former life. Hell no. They would never find someone willing to take a chance on loving them. Did you know that she called me the very first day that she met you? She believed she fell in love with you at first sight. I then asked her if she planned on telling you about her past, and her reply was no. She asked, why should I tell him? He will never know."

"But instead, she lied. She lied about her parents, about her little sister, and about herself. She knew I really loved her, and I believed she really loved me. Shouldn't love make you tell the truth? I deserved the truth." Isaiah finished his drink.

Peppa placed her drink back onto the table. "Isaiah, look at it from her point of view. How was she going to tell you that her father hated her because she grew up gay? Or that her parents threw her out of their house at sixteen because they didn't understand her sexuality? That she was forbidden to see her little sister again, the only person who genuinely loved and mattered to her. Would you have understood that, Isaiah? It took years for her to accept the unnecessary separation from her sister. I helped her legally change her name to Nicole, hoping that wearing her sister's name would fill the void and keep her sister's memory with her. Would you have understood that, Isaiah? It is important that you understand why she refused to tell you about her past. You offered her a chance to validate the woman she had become. She found true love with you. You were finally the answer for all the sacrifices she'd made. There was no way she would jeopardize losing you, and that was her reason for not telling you the truth."

"Can I see her, please?" he asked.

"She's not here. She went to her sister's funeral."

"Isaiah looked at his watch. It was 10:39 A.M."

# THIRTEEN

Nicole solemnly walked up the concrete steps that led to the center, double-door entrance of the St. Hope Baptist Church.

The man standing at the huge, solid oak doors smiled softly at her.

Once she ascended the steps, she looked at him.

He recognized her face and quickly looked at the obituary. He handed her an obituary.

"Are you her twin sister?" he asked.

"No, I was her brother." She closed her eyes and took a deep breath.

She then walked into the crowded church foyer, oblivious to the people pointing and staring at her. She felt her heart beating visibly beneath the simple yet flattering black dress and matching black heels. She clutched her small black purse hanging from her right shoulder. Her hair was worn in a simple, classic French twist in the back.

She entered the church sanctuary and proceeded down the center aisle.

In the center of the church, in front of the alter she saw a soft pink casket.

Nicole felt her knees give way. She quickly caught hold of a pew and steadied herself.

People from the foyer followed her into the church. Several people attending the service noticed her, and some of them even stood up. One woman squealed, which caused Nicole's mother to look back.

Elizabeth Bennett slowly stood up from her seat in the first pew. In disbelief, her hands unconsciously covered her mouth as fresh tears fell from her eyes.

Nicole did not see her mother; she remained focused on the casket.

Her mother began walking towards her in hopes of intercepting Nicole before she made it to the casket.

Nicole walked past her mother and stood before the casket.

Elizabeth could not muster the courage to embrace her child.

Nicole gazed into Kyla's beautiful pink casket, adorned with numerous elaborate floral arrangements.

"No," Nicole said as emotions consumed her. She reached for the casket as she became lightheaded. She missed the casket and fell to the floor, crying uncontrollably.

Everyone attending the funeral stood up.

Nicole felt a hand gently touch her shoulder.

"You are far too beautiful to be on the floor. Can you try to stand up?" he whispered in her ear.

Through watery eyes, Nicole looked up and saw her father.

Tears were also flowing from his eyes.

She placed her hand in his, and he lovingly assisted her to her feet. She threw her arms around his neck and cried.

He cried with her.

Her mother fainted as people rushed to her, including the pastor.

"I'm so sorry," he said in her ear.

She released her father and firmly held on to the casket.

Her father held her right hand for support.

Outside of the stitches concealed with makeup that ran across her sister's forehead, Kyla resembled a sleeping angel, Nicole thought to herself.

"Hi, Yammy," she spoke quietly. "You look so beautiful. I knew you would be." She leaned forward toward her sister lying in the casket.

"Did you know that I never stopped loving you? I'm so sorry," she cried. "I am so sorry that I wasn't here for you. I didn't try hard enough to keep you in my life. You mean the world to me, the only reason that I'm alive today. Because I knew... I knew that I would get the chance to see you again. Everyone at home calls me Nicole. I had my name changed. My name reminds me of how much you mean to me."

She kissed her sister's cheek.

"Every day I thought of how it was going to be when we saw each other again. What am I supposed to do now?" she cried.

"Yammy, I need to hear you say my name. Please, just one more time, say Jonnie, okay? Please, Yammy! Please!!!"

"Come on, baby, you need to come and sit down." Her father attempted to pull her away from the coffin.

Nicole held on tightly. "Yammy, please help me!"

"Sweetheart, it's okay, please come and sit down." "No. Yammy!"

"You're going to hurt yourself. Come and sit down, please."

Nicole looked around and realized where she was.

She released her sister's casket.

People started walking towards her and trying to console her.

Her father held her firmly by the waist.

Everyone crowded around her.

She couldn't breathe.

"No. I can't stay here. I have to leave." She tried to pull away from her father.

He refused to let her go.

"Just relax, everything is going to be okay. I know that you're hurting. Please come and sit down."

"No, please, I want to leave. Please, let me go."

"I promise, I won't let anything happen to you. Just relax."

"Please let me go, I have to leave."

"It's okay, sir, I will take care of her," he said to Nicole's father.

William Bennett looked at the young man.

"She will be fine with me."

Nicole faced Isaiah.

"Come with me, Nicole. I will get you out of here." He extended his hand to her.

She took his hand. "It's okay, I got you. You ready?"

Isaiah wrapped his arm around her waist, and they exited the church.

# FOURTEEN

Isaiah escorted Nicole through the full church parking lot. He reached inside his pants pocket to retrieve the rental car key. He unlocked and opened the passenger door for Nicole. "Take it nice and slow."

He assisted her into the car. He then reached across her and fastened her seat belt. He closed the passenger door for her.

"Excuse me, young man."

Isaiah turned around. He recognized Nicole's father; he could see the family resemblance. "How are you doing, sir?" Isaiah said.

They shook hands firmly.

"I'm fine under the circumstances. My name is William Bennett. How are you?

"I'm good. I am Isaiah Mathis. I offer my condolences."

"Yes, thank you. Her mother is taking it pretty hard. She was a great kid." Mr. Bennett glanced at Nicole sitting in the car. "What is her name?"

"Nicole. She named herself after her sister."

"How do you know my... my child?" William asked uneasily.

"She is.... she was my...she is my friend," Isaiah responded uneasily.

"Do you two reside in San Diego, Mr. Mathis?"

"No, sir, we live in Atlanta. That is where I met her."

"I assume that you two have accommodations here in San Diego, somewhere, yes?"

"Yes, sir, we are staying in Hillcrest at the Hillcrest Suites."

"Good, her mother and I were wondering if perhaps we can sit down and talk with our... child, if that's okay?"

"Sir, that's up to her. I'm going to take her to the room and try to calm her down. She has been through a lot this week." Isaiah reached into his back pocket and removed his wallet.

He handed Mr. Bennett one of his business cards. "This is my card. It has my new cell number written on the back. We are in the Hillcrest Suites, Room 246, registered in my name. If you will excuse me, I really need to get her to lie down."

"Sure, son, I understand. Take care of her, and expect to hear from me soon."

"Nice meeting you, Mr. Bennett."

"Same here, talk to you later." Isaiah walked around the rear of the car to the driver's side.

He got in and closed the door. He simply smiled at Nicole. "You feeling alright?"

She struggled to respond.

He placed his left finger gently over her lips. "Shhhh, we can talk later. I'm so glad to see you again." He reached into the glove compartment and handed her a small box of Kleenex. "Let me get you outta here."

# FIFTEEN

N icole's eyes slowly fluttered open. She gradually focused on her new surroundings. It appeared to be a hotel room, she assumed.

She felt Isaiah cuddled close behind her, with his massive arm around her waist.

"You awake?" he asked softly in her ear.

She felt his masculinity stirring against her rear end.

"Yes," she responded, still feeling some kind of way about him being near her.

"You were sleeping awhile; you feel better?"

"A little."

"You hungry?" he repeatedly ground his rapidly growing manhood against her soft buttocks.

"Yes." She pushed back against him, falling right back into their familiarity with each other for comfort.

"I missed you, baby," he whispered in her ear.

"I missed you, too."

He let loose her hair from the French twist as he tenderly licked and nibbled at her ear. He masterfully glided his large hands to her breasts and began to massage them. He assertively sucked on her neck as he pulled her dress up past her hips. He reached for her panties.

She grabbed his hand.

"Isaiah, I can't." She attempted to rise from the bed.

He locked his arm around her waist.

"What's wrong?" he asked.

Nicole was confused; she desperately yearned to surrender her body to Isaiah, yet her mind was telling her no. "I'm just not sure that..."

"I'm sure."

"I don't think..."

"Don't think, just let it happen."

"Isaiah, please," she begged.

He released his grip on her.

Nicole sat up on the edge of the bed. "I just don't feel comfortable right now, I'm sorry." She stood up, disappeared into the bathroom, and turned on the faucet.

Isaiah quickly grabbed his cell phone and dialed Malik.

"Hey, man, can you talk?" he whispered into the phone.

"What's up, dude? Why are you whispering? You got Nicole?"

"Yeah, she's in the bathroom. I got to be quick. I'm about to hit it, just to see if there is a difference now that I know what time it is."

"Handle it then."

"I'm out." He ended the call.

A few minutes later, Isaiah knocked gently on the bathroom door. "You aw'ight in there?"

"I'm fine." She rinsed her face with warm water.

"Can I come in?"

She opened the door as she dried off her face.

Isaiah was not wearing a shirt.

"You okay?" he asked with genuine concern. He saw that she was still stunning, even with the fading bruises.

"I guess so. So much has happened in this last week, I think we need to talk."

"Talk about what? Your life before you met me? Peppa opened my eyes to your situation. I'm sorry about your childhood, your sister, and I'm sorry about what I did to you. What else is there to talk about?"

"What about us, Isaiah?"

"What about us?" He stood close, face to face. "I'm here because you needed me. And I'm sure you would be there for me if I needed you. Nothing else matters."

"So where do we go from here?" she questioned.

"I can show you better than I can tell you." He kissed her deeply on the mouth.

She dropped the towel, and she opened her mouth to receive his tongue as she wrapped her arms around his neck.

He lifted her off the floor as she wrapped her legs around his waist. He carried her to the bed and gently laid her down. He swiftly removed her dress. He then took off his slacks and boxers in one fluid motion.

She removed her panties and bra.

He mounted her as they shared a passionate kiss.

She spread her legs apart to accommodate Isaiah's length and girth into her hot, wet, anxious vagina.

He pushed his throbbing, rigid penis inside of her until he felt his scrotum touch her buttocks. He gently pulled out and re-entered her repeatedly until he found his rhythm. He tenderly bit at her neck as she moaned softly.

"Yes," she moaned. "Make love to me, Isaiah. Take it, it's yours."

Her sexually explicit comments intensified with each stroke of Isaiah's massive manhood.

"Please, fuck me, Isaiah. Fuck me, please." He forcefully rammed his ebony shaft into her eager flesh. His eyes are locked onto hers.

Tears stream down the sides of her face. She can no longer speak because it feels so good to reconnect with him. She could only release high-pitched wails as she thrust her pelvis forward in sync with his rhythm.

"You like that? You want it? Yeah, yeah, yeah..." he chanted, panting heavily with each thrust as he continually drilled her mercilessly.

Then they both cried out in climactic orgasm as he pumped ropes of thick, white semen into her.

She milked every drop of his fluid.

He collapsed on the side of her.

Both were breathing heavily, but neither of them could speak.

He hurriedly got out of bed and rushed into the bathroom.

# Sixteen

" Thank you for coming. This meant a lot to us." William said as he closed the front door behind the last of their guests.

He thought they would never leave. He glanced around the living room and formal dining area.

"I hope she doesn't expect me to help her clean this up," he thought quietly to himself." He began picking up used dishes and silverware and taking them into the kitchen.

The enormous kitchen was in worse shape than the rest of the house.

He decided it would be much easier to check on Elizabeth. He marched up the carpeted staircase and stood in the doorway of their bedroom.

She was sound asleep.

He stood over her and watched her sleep peacefully.

She is such a beautiful woman, he thought to himself.

He sat down carefully, cautious not to wake her from a much-needed slumber.

He remembered the first day he laid eyes on Elizabeth.

They were both attending San Diego State College. He was a

senior and she a freshman. He knew that she would be the mother of his children. Lovingly gazing at her, he noticed that she hadn't changed much in their thirty-two years of marriage.

Most of the people their age were overweight and out of shape, including himself.

He developed a taste for imported beer during the football season, basketball season, baseball season, and occasional tennis tournaments when the William sisters were playing. But not his Elizabeth, she improved with age.

He softly stroked her colored hair as her almond-shaped eyes fluttered open.

"I'm sorry, I didn't mean to wake you. You look so beautiful lying here," William apologized.

"I needed to get up. Has everyone left?" She sat up.

"Yes, they're gone. How are you feeling?"

"I don't think the pain will ever go away. I do feel better after that nap," she smiled. "How long was I out?"

"Almost three hours. You needed it."

"How bad is it downstairs?"

"It's pretty bad."

"I guess I'd better get up and get started."

"Let me give you a hand."

"Thank you, William, but I can handle it. Besides, it will give me something to do." She kissed him on the cheek.

"What was that for?" he asked.

"Do I have to give an explanation every time I give you a kiss? Thank you for really being here for me." She walked down the stairs.

"Hey, she was my daughter too." He followed behind her.

She surveyed the damage in the lower portion of the house.

"This is going to take forever." She began picking up the glasses and dishes, and William did as well. "William, you don't have to help; I can handle it."

He predicted she would say that. He followed her into the kitchen.

"It would be a pleasure to help my wife." He smiled.

"Thank you." She smiled back at her husband.

"I will get the rest of the dishes out of the living room."

"And I will start in the kitchen." She began rinsing the dishes and placed them in the dishwasher.

William came into the kitchen with another stack of dishes. "Where do you want these?"

"You can set those on the counter. I'll get to them in a moment. What am I supposed to do with all this food?"

"Eat it. You can make me a plate now."

"I should have known better than to ask you." She smiled. "Greedy."

William walked back into the living room, glancing at the wall lined with framed pictures of his daughter at various stages of her life.

There were several pictures of him and his daughter together. He became conscious that there were no pictures of Jonathan. He continued gathering dishes and strolled back into the kitchen. His wife is seated in one of the dining room chairs, her head down.

Elizabeth was crying.

He placed the dishes into the sink.

"You okay, Beth?" He lovingly stroked her shoulder.

"I was thinking about Jonathan. It breaks my heart to imagine all the pain he must be feeling. I know he must hate us for what we did. I love my son. When he walked into the funeral like that, I couldn't take it."

He knelt in front of her.

"We did the best we could. I couldn't deal with him at all. But seeing him today forced me to reconsider. All those years, I tried to make him more of a man, more like me. I was so selfish, I only thought of myself and what people thought of me with a homosexual son. If I had known he could grow up and become the person he is now, I would have been much more supportive."

"Were we to encourage that type of behavior? How do you raise a son who wants to change his sex?"

"Elizabeth, we did what we thought was best. Jonathan is going to have to accept that, and we're going to have to accept the fact that he is now a she. And that he was going to be a she no matter how we dealt with him."

"What can we possibly say so that he will forgive us? Kyla meant so much to him. You don't know how bad I felt when I saw him walking towards the casket. I want to talk to my child, William, and explain our side of the story. I will beg for forgiveness."

"We both will."

"Does he... she live here? Did you get her phone number?"

"They are in the Hillcrest Suites."

"Who is that man she left with? Was that her friend?"

"His name is Isaiah Mathis. He said they are good friends. They live in Atlanta. I have his business card." He retrieved it from his shirt pocket.

"He is a mechanic with two locations. I'm not sure what she does."

He handed his card to his wife. "What is her name?"

"Nicole. She wears her sister's middle name. I didn't get her last name."

"I need to talk to my child. Will you please call them now?"

"Beth, it's almost eleven o'clock at night. I will call them first thing in the morning."

"No, please, call them now. Please."

William stood up and grabbed the cordless kitchen phone.

He dialed 411.

"Hello, can I have the number to the Hillcrest Suites in Hillcrest? Thank you."

He pressed 1 to be instantly connected.

"Hello, yes, I'm trying to reach a Mr. Isaiah Mathis. I believe he is in room 246. "

"Just one moment," the operator said. "Hold on, please, and I will connect you."

"Thank you."

The phone rang in his ear.

# SEVENTEEN

Isaiah called Malik from his cell phone. "Hello? What up, man?"

"What up, Dawg?" Malik answered cheerfully. "You got my girl?"

"She's right next to me," he answered proudly.

"Well, put her on the phone, fool. Hey, Michelle," Malik yelled. "He got Nicole, pick up the phone."

"Hi, Malik."

"What's up, sweetheart? How are you doing? I heard about your sister."

"Hello, hello...." Michelle interrupted.

"Hi, Michelle."

"Nicole! Girl, I miss you."

"I miss you too, Michelle."

"I'm sorry about your sister; I didn't even know you had a sister. Are you okay?"

"I'm fine, now that Isaiah is here with me."

"So, when are you coming home?" Michelle asked.

Nicole looked up at Isaiah.

"Tell her we will be back in Atlanta tomorrow, early evening," Isaiah said.

"He said tomorrow, early evening."

"Girl, I can't wait."

"Neither can I, Michelle. I love you."

"I love you too."

"How are you two getting home from the airport? We can come get you." Malik asked.

"You need to discuss that with Isaiah. I love you, Malik, and I appreciate both of you being there for Isaiah and me. Thank you."

"We love you too," they said in unison.

"Hold on, here's Isaiah." Nicole handed him the cell phone.

"Hello?"

"Hi, Isaiah."

"Hey, Michelle, I told you I would get her back."

"Well, you better hurry up and bring her back home."

"I will. I called to let you know that she is with me, and everything is fine."

"I love you, Isaiah."

"I love you too, Michelle."

"Hey Dawg, how y'all getting home from the airport? We can meet you there."

"That's cool. Let me get the tickets...We're on Delta, flight 1065, arriving at Hartsfield at 6:39 P.M. You got that?"

"Bet. See you tomorrow."

"Thanks, man."

"Not a problem, love you, Dawg." Isaiah hung up.

The hotel room phone rang.

Isaiah answered the phone as Nicole stared at him curiously.

"Hello?"

"Hello, Isaiah, this is William Bennett. Sorry to call you this late."

"How are you doing, sir?" he responded.

"We are both doing fine. I hope I am not calling too late. My wife and I were wondering if we may have a word with our child."

"Who is it?" Nicole asked.

Isaiah covered the receiver with his hand. "It's your parents. They want to talk to you."

Nicole shook her head no and got out of bed. "Mr. Bennett, can you hold on a minute, please?"

"Sure," William responded.

Isaiah got up out of bed and followed Nicole to the bathroom.

"What did he say?" Elizabeth questioned.

"He asked me to hold on."

Isaiah stood in front of the closed bathroom door. "They want to talk to you."

"I have nothing to say to those people."

"They are your parents. You should at least listen to what they have to say."

"I don't care about what they have to say."

"We leave tomorrow afternoon. You will never have to see them again. Just hear what they have to say, tonight."

"Isaiah, I don't want to talk to them. Can we leave it at that?" Nicole turned on the shower.

"Okay." He picked up the phone. "Hello? Mr. Bennett?"

"Yes, I'm here."

"She says she doesn't want to talk."

"Tell her she doesn't have to talk. All she has to do is listen."

Elizabeth took the phone from her husband.

"Hello, Isaiah, this is Elizabeth. I know that... she is terribly upset right now. Maybe tomorrow she'll feel more like talking. I know this is extremely hard for her; it is for all of us dealing with this painful tragedy. Hopefully, after a night's rest, she will reconsider. Then the two of you will join us for breakfast or lunch, where we can sit and talk."

"Ma'am, our flight leaves tomorrow afternoon, and we plan to spend tomorrow with a friend of hers. I'm sorry."

"You can't leave tomorrow. I must speak with my child. Please, I beg you, somehow persuade my child to speak with us." She started crying. "I'm so sorry."

William took the phone from his wife and sat her at the kitchen table.

Isaiah could hear him trying to console her. "Hello, Isaiah, sorry about that," he said.

"No problem."

"You two are leaving tomorrow?"

"Yes, sir."

"You can't leave tomorrow."

"We already have tickets, Mr. Bennett."

"I know that you aren't familiar with my wife and me. And I don't know what our child has told you about us, but we really do love our child. We tried to raise him the best we could. Will you please help us, Isaiah?"

"Sir, what can I do?"

That was the first time he had ever heard anyone address Nicole as him. He didn't know how to react.

"You can start by calling me Will."

"Will, what do you want me to do?"

"Could you take a later flight? I will pay for the tickets, first class."

"She wants to go home."

"When do you check out of the hotel?"

"Check out is at 11:00 A.M."

"What if we met you in the parking lot of the hotel at 11:00 A.M.? Would you do that for us?"

"I can do that."

"Well, then it's done. We will see both of you tomorrow morning." William said happily.

"Have a good night."

# EIGHTEEN

"You made sure you got everything, Isaiah?" Nicole asked.

"I'm sure. I already put my luggage in the trunk. Damn, I'm going to miss this view. San Diego is a beautiful city. Let's go." He closed the door behind them, and they headed for the elevators.

They walked to the front desk to return the hotel room key.

"I hope you had a pleasant stay here in the Suites." The front desk clerk said.

"Very nice, thank you," Isaiah responded.

"Next time you're in San Diego, I hope you will come back and stay with us again."

"We will." Isaiah wrapped his arm around Nicole and escorted her out of the hotel lobby towards the rental car.

As they approached the rental car, Nicole stopped walking. She saw her parents waiting up ahead.

They walked towards her.

"Good morning, don't you look beautiful today." Mr. Bennett spoke, focused intently on Nicole.

"How you doing, Will?" Isaiah said, extending his hand to Mr. Bennett.

They shook hands.

Nicole frowned at Isaiah.

"Good morning, Mrs. Bennett." She was also focused on Nicole.

She smiled at Isaiah.

"Good morning, Isaiah. Good morning, Nicole."

"Isaiah, will you please let me in the car?" Nicole said, ignoring her parents.

"Nicole, they are speaking to you."

"Isaiah, please."

Elizabeth walked up to Nicole. "I'm so deeply sorry. I know that doesn't help you."

"You're right, it doesn't." She quickly walked past her parents towards the car door.

"What was I supposed to do, Jonathan?" Elizabeth cried out.

Nicole froze. She looked at Isaiah.

"How do you raise a son who wants to become your daughter?"

William wrapped his arm around his wife for support.

"This was not a common issue when you two were growing up. There weren't any support groups or family counselors. What was I supposed to do? Who was I going to talk to? There isn't an instruction manual for raising children. I did what I thought was best for both of you. You were my first child. I prayed it was just a phase you were going through, having to explain it to everyone, including your father. I guess I was in denial. What was I supposed to do?"

Nicole faced her mother. "You could have tried loving me."

"I did love you. Do you know how hard it was for me to put my child, my firstborn, on the streets? Your sister found out and never forgave me for that."

"And I can't forgive you either."

"We tried to find you. We hired a private investigator, and we searched all over America. Jonathan Lamont Bennett no longer existed. We thought you had died. Do you know how long I have been suffering? Now, whenever I walk into your sister's old bedroom, I feel as though I have lost both of my children."

"You took the only person away from me on this earth who loved me unconditionally. She never cared about who I was or what I wanted to be. She loved me for me, and you took her away. Both of you."

"Please, don't do this," she pleaded. "I can't bear losing you again."

"Please, look into your heart and try to forgive us," her father added.

"I can't, you buried my heart yesterday." Nicole turned away as Isaiah held the car door open for her.

"She wrote letters to you."

Nicole froze.

"She wrote letters to you all the time. As a girl, Kyla would pray every night that I would find you and give her letters to you."

Elizabeth reached inside her purse and retrieved a handful of letters.

"Here, these belong to you. I couldn't fit them all inside my purse." She held out the letters to Nicole. "I have a box of them at home, and I'd be more than willing to send them to you."

Nicole turned around to face her parents. She slowly walked towards her parents, gazing intently at the letters her mother held out to her. She gently took the letters from her mother's hand and clutched them to her chest.

Nicole pulled one of the letters loose and read her former name written in crayon. Tears fell from the corners of her eyes.

"I have a big box of them at home," Elizabeth cried to her.

Isaiah embraced Nicole.

She cried into his chest.

"You want your letters, Nicole?" Isaiah whispered in her ear.

Nicole shook her head yes into Isaiah's chest.

"I guess we will follow you to your house, Will." Isaiah assisted Nicole into the rental car.

She carefully laid the letters across her lap. She picked up the first letter written in crayon. She removed it from the envelope.

As she unfolded it, a picture of the two of them as children fell out. In the picture, Jonathan is around seven years old because an infant, Kyla, is asleep in his arms. She read the letter.........

Jonnie,

Where are you? Why did you leave? Mommie said you ran away. Did I do something wrong? Please come back home. We miss you very much.

yammy

Nicole carefully refolded the letter and placed it into its proper envelope.

She read the next letter, also written in crayon.

Jonathan I am so
sad, Please come back.
I am not happy anymore
Mommie won't let me
Sleep in your room.
I need you.

                    Yammy

Jonnie.
     Please come home.
We miss you. Don't you
miss me and momie? Do
you have another sister?
Does she love you more
than me?

                    Yammy

Hi Johnathan

I t's me yammy.
Mommy and I are
so sad. We miss you
very much. I thought
I saw you at my
School today. We have
a phone. Please call
me. Mommy can't read
betime stories like you.
Your little sister

Kila
Yammy

Jonathan

Are you mad
at me? I am sorry
Please come back home.
Mommie cant read
bedtime stories like you.
Did I see you at my
School today?
                Yammy

Jonathon,

Hurry and come home.
We are moving away
and you might not be
able to find us.
Please hurry.

Kyla

(Yammy)

By the time Nicole read the last letter, they were pulling into her parents' driveway.

Isaiah parked behind Will's smoky gray Mercedes-Benz as he opened the electric garage door.

Her parents got out of the car.

Isaiah got out of the car and walked around to Nicole's side. "You ready?"

She placed her hand in his.

"Please, come in." William opened the door inside the garage.

Elizabeth has already entered the house. "Let me show you the house." William invited them in.

This wasn't the house Nicole remembered growing up in.

"Your mother said she could no longer live in the old house, too many bad memories."

Nicole and Isaiah walked into the den, which was to the left of the kitchen.

The room was warm and inviting, complete with a small fireplace.

William closed the door behind them. "Let me give the two of you the grand tour," he smiled at Nicole.

They followed William through the large, graceful house as he explained the origins of certain furniture, artifacts, and collectibles.

Isaiah was impressed by the backyard's size and landscaping, as well as by William's sports room and sports memorabilia.

He ended the tour in their elegant, spacious all-white living room.

The entire room is decorated in white, the draperies, furniture, and a small, white baby grand piano. "Please, have a seat."

Nicole and Isaiah sat next to each other on the expensive, white leather couch.

"You have a beautiful home, Mr. Bennett," Isaiah said.

"Thank you, son. Make sure you say that to my wife because she spent a lot of my money to hear those very words."

Isaiah laughed in agreement.

"Can I get you something to drink? Have you two eaten breakfast? I make a mean western omelet."

"No. Thank you, we ate at the hotel," Isaiah answered.

"Well, I think I am going to have myself a second cup of coffee. Would you care to join me, young man?"

"Sure, why not?" Isaiah decided to let Nicole be alone with her mother.

"Would you like a cup of coffee, Nicole?" her father smiled softly.

She shook her head no.

The men left the room.

Nicole was left alone in her parents' house, and she felt surreal — like she did not belong here. She gazed at several large, framed portraits of her sister Kyla hanging on the walls. She stood up and walked to the wall. This must be her yearbook picture, Nicole assumed. Then there is a picture of her and a handsome young man.

"It is amazing how much the two of you look alike," Elizabeth said.

Nicole was startled by her mother's voice behind her. She spun around to face her.

"I'm sorry, I didn't mean to interrupt you." Nicole took her seat back on the couch.

"Did you see this one? It's my favorite."

Elizabeth gently lifted the exquisite, silver-framed portrait, replaced the mantel, and handed it to Nicole. It was Kyla's wedding picture. She was breathtaking.

"Wasn't she beautiful?"

"Yes, she was."

"I want you to see her bedroom. It's exactly the same way she left it when she went away to college. Would you like to see it?"

"Yes." Elizabeth extended her hand to Nicole. Nicole rose from the couch without her mother's assistance. She followed her mother upstairs to her sister's bedroom.

Her mother stood to the side of the closed door. "Please, go ahead."

Nicole took hold of the doorknob and tenderly opened the door.

The first thing that caught her eye was a giant poster-sized picture of her former self that hung over her sister's bed. Her walls were littered with pictures of a youthful, jubilant Jonathan Bennett. There were photos of past Christmases and birthdays (his and hers), trips to the park, Disneyland, Magic Mountain, The San

Diego Zoo, his and her first day of school, and Jonathan reading bedtime stories to her.

Nicole started crying. She stood at the foot of her sister's pink, queen-sized bed.

The bed was adorned in pink and white with a Betty Boop comforter and matching shams. Her bedroom furniture is white, accented with a pink telephone, pink lampshades, and a pink computer. Kyla even had a pink 32" television. She could almost see her teenage sister stretched across the bed, talking on the telephone.

She felt her knees getting weak. She needed to sit down. She sat on the footstool at the foot of her sister's bed.

Her mother walked into the room and opened her double-door closet.

Inside the closet on the right, partially hidden, sat three large cardboard boxes.

Her mother took down the top box and placed it at Nicole's feet.

"These are the letters she wrote to you." Her mother opened the box. "She wrote you nearly every day for a couple of years. Then she would write you only at Christmas and on your birthday. Then all of a sudden, she quit writing letters to you. She started writing to you and God in her diary. Her diary is in her nightstand."

Her mother retrieved the diary and handed it to her. "I want you to have this too."

Nicole clutched the diary to her chest. "Thank you."

Her mother returned to the closet and removed a second, larger box. She placed it on top of the box with the letters. "These are all your Christmas presents and birthday gifts that she paid for with her money. She wrapped them all herself."

Elizabeth opened the box. They were all wonderfully preserved and beautifully decorated in a variety of shades of pink.

Nicole became overwhelmed and cried openly.

Her mother cried with her.

She handed Nicole a box of tissues and then wiped her own tears away.

"Hello... hello... Mom, where are you?" He yelled at the foot of the carpeted staircase.

"We're in here." Elizabeth blew her nose.

They heard footsteps ascending the staircase and down the hall coming towards the bedroom.

"Whose car is that in the driveway?" He walked into the bedroom.

He looked at Nicole.

He walked up to her. "I saw you at the funeral yesterday. It is so nice to finally meet you. Hello, my name is Gregory. Do you know your sister loved you very much? She would talk about you for hours. I was afraid she wouldn't marry me because we didn't have your blessing." He smiled. "I'm sorry, what is your name?"

"Hi, I'm Nicole." She recognized him from the wedding picture.

He gently shook her hand. "What a pleasure to finally meet you. It's too bad that they are under such horrible circumstances. I'm your sister's husband. I've heard so many wonderful things about you. It's quite obvious that you two were sisters."

He hugged his mother-in-law. "How are you feeling today, Mom?"

"I'm hanging in there."

A little boy walked around the corner and into the room, carrying a small bag of cheddar-flavored Goldfish.

They all focused on him.

He saw Nicole and let his bag of goldfish fall to the floor. Without saying a word, he walked straight to Nicole. He touched her knee as his bottom lip began to quiver.

No one said a word.

Nicole could sense that he wanted to hug her. "Hello," she whispered, fighting back tears. "And what is your name?"

"Jonathan."

Nicole couldn't resist and swept her little nephew into her arms.

He hugged her back.

"That is your Auntie, Nicole. She is your mother's sister," his father explained.

"My mommy died," Jonathan said sadly.

"Yes, I know.

That's why I'm here."

Jonathan smiled at Nicole. "Do you live with Grammy now?" he asked with enthusiasm.

"No, I live in Atlanta."

"You look like my mommy."

"Yes, I know," she smiled.

"Where is Atlanta? Daddy, can we go to Atlanta with Auntie Nicole?"

"What about your Grammy?" Gregory asked.

Nicole released him, and Jonathan ran over to Elizabeth.

Elizabeth knelt as Jonathan ran into her arms.

"Hi, Grammy." Jonathan kissed her on the cheek. "Grammy can go with us, too," he said excitedly.

They all laughed.

"You'll have to ask Auntie Nicole," Gregory said. Jonathan ran back to Nicole.

"Can we come live with you, Auntie Nicole, in Atlanta?" Jonathan stood in front of Nicole, touching her knee.

"Jonathan, we can't live with Auntie Nicole, but we can go for a visit." His father explained.

"Can we come, Auntie Nicole?"

"Of course, you can." Jonathan hugged her.

"You all can." She smiled at Gregory and her mother.

Gregory hugged Elizabeth as she cried into his chest.

William and Isaiah walked into the room. "What's going on in here?"

Elizabeth rushed into her husband's arms.

Nicole stood up, holding Jonathan.

Jonathan was staring at Isaiah.

Nicole walked over to Isaiah.

"Isaiah, I want you to meet my nephew, Jonathan. Jonathan, this is Isaiah."

"Hi, Isaiah."

"What's up, little man?" Isaiah shook his little hand.

"Hi, Grampy Will." Jonathan reached for his grandfather.

"How is my favorite Grandson?" Jonathan hugged his grandfather.

"Guess what, Grampy Will? We can all go to Atlanta to visit Auntie Nicole." Jonathan looked at Isaiah. "Isaiah, you can come too."

They all laughed.

"Well, thank you, little man, good looking out." Isaiah high-fived Jonathan.

Isaiah introduced himself to Gregory. "How you doing man? Isaiah Mathis."

They shook hands.

"I'm hanging in there. I'm Gregory Thompson, nice to meet you. Kyla was my wife. Welcome to the family."

"Thanks, man." Isaiah turned his attention to Elizabeth. "You have a beautiful home, Mrs. Bennett."

"Thank you, Isaiah. Did my husband tell you to say that to me?"

"Well, let's go downstairs, where we can talk," William said, before Isaiah could respond. "This room makes me sad."

William carried Jonathan out of the room.

Gregory and Elizabeth followed them out. Nicole hugged Isaiah.

"Now, I can see why you love pink so much," Isaiah observed.

"Grampy, wait."

"What is it, Jonathan?"

"Put me down."

William lowered Jonathan down on the carpeted hallway floor. "I want to go get Auntie Nicole."

Jonathan ran past Gregory and Elizabeth back into the room. He took Nicole by the hand. "Come on, Auntie Nicole."

Jonathan pulled Nicole with him out of the room as Isaiah followed behind them.

Isaiah looked back into the room at the adolescent boy's posters on the wall.

# NINETEEN

After reading her sister's letters, Nicole felt the deep bond they once shared.

The letters began as Yammy, the heartbroken, abandoned little ten-year-old girl, and ended as Kyla — the blossoming, free-spirited teenager.

Instead of watching Kyla mature, she was reading it.

She was eternally grateful to her mother for preserving such meaningful memories.

"I just read the last letter." She said to Isaiah, seated next to her in first class.

Isaiah was in deep thought, staring out of the airplane window. He couldn't get the little boy's picture out of his mind. The reality of the situation came crashing in.

Regardless of Nicole's captivating natural beauty and presence, he witnessed photographic proof that she was born he. He was angry and confused. *Does this make me gay? Hell no. She is a woman in every sense of the word,* he thought to himself. *Knowing the truth is what got me fucked up. That magazine fucked up my life.*

"Isaiah."

He turned in his seat to face Nicole. "What's up?"

"I tried to tell you I finished the last letter."

"What did it say?"

"The letters weren't really in order when I began reading them, basically, that she had outgrown writing such childish letters. Elizabeth said she continued to write me in her diary. So, I guess I will start reading this next. Are you okay?" She could tell something was bothering him.

"That *Connections* magazine, how long did you do that? Why would you do that?"

"My parents threw me out at sixteen. I didn't know what else to do. I was young, hungry, and on the streets. To get a job, you need a home address and a phone number. I had neither. And when you look like a teenage runaway girl, that's what you get. I was thankful to meet Peppa when I did. My life could have ended up much worse."

"So, when did you start advertising in the *Connection*?"

"I hated prostitution, and when I moved in with Peppa, I got a real job. I worked at a grocery store and was promoted twice. First to lead cashier, and then to vault accounting. Then management found out that I was transitioning, and I lost my job. Transitioning means you're in the process of changing sexes, undergoing hormonal therapy, and living as a woman every day. I was barely making enough money to pay bills and for my doctor visits and medications. That's when I started escorting. I am so sorry you had to find out that way. I honestly believed no one would ever find out about the old me."

"No one else knows about you, except Malik and me."

"And whoever left that envelope."

"Whoever it was, they knew about our upcoming marriage. Who would want to do that? Is there anyone out to get you?"

"Not that I know of. What about you?"

"I thought about my ex, Yvonne, my son's mother. But how

would she know about you? And on top of that, why would she care? She got married while I was locked up."

"Wait a minute, I think I know who it is. It could be Brock Bass."

"Brock Bass?" Isaiah questioned. "The old quarterback from the Los Angeles Quakes, Brock Bass? The famous, two-time MVP of pro football who owns all the sports bars and nightclubs from L.A. to New York. You know 'BB'?"

"I met Brock through the *Southern California Connections*."

"Did he know that you were a......?"

"Yes, he met me that way."

"Like you are now?"

"No. I didn't have my sexual reassignment surgery. He was against the final surgery. But in the end, he was the one who paid for it. He knew how much it meant to me."

"So, Brock is gay?"

"I don't know. He never explored that side of my sexuality. I think he was impressed with the fact that no one could detect my true sex or would even question it, for that matter. In our special friendship, he insisted on making me perfect. He became obsessed with me."

"How long were you together?"

"Brock is a very married man, so we were never together. He handled our unique friendship with the utmost discretion. He totally changed my life. He set me up in a small, secluded three-bedroom house in a suburb of San Diego, in which I could have no visitors. He supported me in every way, even bought me a small car so I could have transportation."

"Why would he want to get to you now?"

"Brock became extremely possessive, to the point of violence. He claimed he owned me because he created me. That's when I decided to leave California to find a new life for the new me. Brock may not be responsible for the envelope, but he's the only person I can think of now who might have done it."

"I need to get some shut-eye before we return home." Isaiah had heard enough. He didn't know if she was telling the truth or if it was another one of her elaborate, twisted lies. He idolized Brock Bass and the game of professional football. He couldn't wait to get home and be rid of this crazy bitch.

"Go ahead, I am going to start reading my sister's diary." She knew things had changed drastically between them, and she understood.

It was apparent when he rescued her from her sister's funeral because after intimacy, he was distant and unaffectionate. His feeble attempt at lovemaking was amateur porn at best.

She knew that her first chance at real love in her new life had ended.

She opened the diary.

This Diary belongs to
Kyla Nicole Bennet. I
dedicate this diary to the
memory of my beloved
brother, Johnathan Jammit
Bennett.

September 16th.

Dear Jonathan,

I pray one day that I
will see you again. It has
been four years since I have
last seen you. Where are you?
What are you doing? Have you
forgotten me? There is not
a day goes by, when I don't
remember you. Sometimes when
I'm at school or walking home
with my friends, I will think I see
you. But it is never you. I
started Junior High School this
week. I attend Parkway Junior

think it hurts her. I feel sorry for mom, she misses you more than I do. I often catch her crying when she is alone. Dad has been coming around alot more since you have been gone. I guess he misses you too.

I guess I should start on my homework now. Junior High is so easy. I love you... Tammy

September 18 . . .

Dear Jonathan,

You would not believe what happened to me at school today. I was having lunch with my friends and this 9th grader, GREGORY THOMPSON walked up to us and asked could he have lunch with me. CAN YOU BELIEVE IT?!!! A NINTH GRADER!!!!! He is so cute not dumb like the rest of the

boys. He said when he grew up,
he was going to be an architect.
that means he wants to build
and design skyscrapers, malls,
mansions, and stuff like that.
He carries around his sketchpad
just like you. I think that's
why I like him because he's
an artist. Just like you. He
asked me what I wanted to
be when I grow up. I told him
a teacher just like you were
to me. I tutor some kids at
school and they are older than
me. I think it's fun helping
other people learn. He purchased
me a chocolate chip cookie
after lunch. And he walked me
home after school. I'm going to
ask mom if I can give him
our phone number, when she
comes home from work. I think
she will like Greeday. I think
you would too. Jonathan. I know
I do. He's tall, brown skinned and
so handsome. He's lanky, but has
nice legs. I saw him at P.E., he

was playing basketball. He's good too! I'd better go and start dinner, so I can surprise mom. that will make it easier for her to say yes, when I ask her to give GREGORY our number. I LOVE YOU.... Yanni

# TWENTY

Nicole and Isaiah exited the plane and headed for the monorail on their concourse.

They boarded the monorail and headed towards the Delta Terminal's baggage claim.

They rode the monorail in silence.

They exited the train and walked toward baggage claim.

"You go ahead and meet Michelle and Malik. I will wait for the luggage," Isaiah said.

"I don't mind. I will wait with you."

"No, go ahead. They're probably waiting for us." "Okay, I'll meet you out front." Nicole walked away from Isaiah, past the baggage claim, and out of the exit doors.

Before she passed through the second set of doors, she spotted Michelle and Malik.

The boys weren't with them.

"NETTIE!!!" Michelle screamed as she jumped up and down, covering her mouth.

"CELIE!!!" Nicole yelled as she ran towards Michelle.

Malik shook his head, laughing as did the other nearby onlookers.

Michelle was the definition of a perfect Georgia peach. She was a shapely, full-figured, natural beauty with flawless, cocoa-brown skin. She was wearing tight black stretch jeans, low-heeled black knee-high boots, and an oversized blouse. Her long, relaxed, jet-black tresses were blowing in the cool fall breeze.

Her handsome husband Malik wore a long-sleeved, thin, pale blue sweater, loose jeans, and caramel-colored Timberlands. He was clean-cut with a neatly tapered goatee, green eyes, and full lips.

Michelle and Nicole embraced tightly as they rocked back and forth.

"Hi, Michelle."

"Hi, Nicole. Girl, I missed you."

"I missed you, too." Michelle took a step back. "Girl, let me look at you. California must have really stressed you out; you look thin. Give me another hug."

They hugged again.

Malik extended his hand to Nicole. "Welcome back, Sweetie."

"Thank you."

Michelle noticed her husband's awkward greeting.

"Where's my boy?" Malik asked Nicole.

"He's waiting for the luggage."

"Y'all go ahead and talk, I'll find Isaiah."

"Thank you for everything, Malik."

"You're welcome," he said and quickly walked away.

"Girl, forgive him, he's been acting strange all day. The boys wanted to come with us to pick you guys up, but he dropped them off at my mother's house." Michelle hugged Nicole again. "It's so good to see you again."

"I love you, Michelle."

"I love you, too."

"We need to talk."

"Yes, we do. What the hell happened between you and Isaiah? They wouldn't tell me anything. Was it that serious?"

"It's pretty bad. Maybe after we get to the house, you and I could go for a drive?"

"Nicole, there is nothing that you can say that I won't understand. I'm your best friend." She held both of Nicole's hands for reassurance.

"Michelle, I don't know how to tell you this…"

"It's okay, girl, what is it?"

"Michelle…I was born male."

Michelle started laughing.

"I know I should have told you in the beginning, but we had gotten so close, so fast, and I…"

"What? Are you serious? Girl, come here." She hugged her tightly. "You're still my sister. You had me fooled. Damn, is that what happened between you and Isaiah? He must have found out."

"Yes, he tried to kill me, that's why I left."

"Damn."

"I don't blame him; he had every right to react the way he did. Michelle, I think the truth destroyed our relationship."

Michelle was at a loss for words. She was in shock. She held onto Nicole to hide her feelings. Michelle thought of what Isaiah must be going through.

"So how does Isaiah feel now?" Michelle asked, looking Nicole directly in the eyes.

"I don't know, he hasn't had much to say to me since we boarded the plane. He did say that the wedding was off, and I understand that."

Michelle nodded in agreement. "Girl, the truth is going to take a little time. I'm so glad that you are both safe at home. It will work out for the best, trust me."

Nicole wasn't so sure.

# TWENTY-ONE

Nicole's heart was pounding as she stood in front of her home.

Malik put his black SUV in reverse and began to roll out of the driveway.

Michelle rolled down the window. "Call me if you need me, girl."

Nicole turned around and smiled at them.

Isaiah had already gone inside with the luggage.

Nicole walked in and stood on the linoleum in the entryway. She was greeted with the same familiar surroundings, but the atmosphere had changed.

The warmth and peace that normally comforted her when she entered her home no longer resided there. It was replaced with tension and uncertainty.

She immediately noticed that all of the pictures of her and Isaiah together were gone.

Nicole looked up the carpeted staircase to the left of the entryway, then to the right at the entrance to the kitchen.

She walked slowly straight ahead into the living room and turned on the light.

The huge, ornate ceiling fan illuminated her spacious, well-furnished living area. The huge, framed portrait of them had been removed as well.

She noticed that he kept all her original, framed drawings up. One by one, she examined her art as if looking at it for the very first time. She tried to put herself back into the frame of mind she was in when she created that particular piece.

She came upon Isaiah's favorite drawing of his son when he was four years old. She walked up close to get a better view of the details she had captured.

Rashidi resembled his father in every way: his rich, dark-brown skin, huge, expressive eyes, and soft, gentle smile.

Nicole couldn't help but smile. She loved Rashidi as though she were his birth mother.

Isaiah quietly walked up behind her. He wanted to touch her, but decided against it. He watched her as she gazed at his favorite portrait.

She was dressed in a pink warm-up suit that belonged to her deceased sister. Her hair was in a simple, yet sexy ponytail that hung seductively between her shoulder blades.

He was so close to her that her fragrance filled his nostrils. He felt his manhood stirring inside his shorts.

He abruptly turned away from her.

Nicole turned around as she saw Isaiah walking away.

He had changed into a white, cotton tank top and navy-blue cut-off sweat shorts.

"Isaiah."

"What up?" He did not turn around because it was visible that she aroused him. "You want something to drink?" He continued to walk into the kitchen.

"Some water, please." She walked to the bar that separated the kitchen from the living room and sat on one of the leather barstools. "You okay? You haven't had much to say to me since we boarded the plane."

He poured her a glass of water and set it in front of her.

"Thank you."

"Yeah."

Nicole took a sip.

He removed a glass from the cabinet, added a few ice cubes, and made himself a stiff drink. He took a healthy swig.

"Isaiah, what's wrong?"

"Everything's wrong. I can't do this. I can't live like this."

"I know. I understand."

"What the fuck do you understand? My head is so fucked up right now. I'm in love with a woman who used to be a man. You have me questioning my manhood and shit. How do you understand that?" He took another swig.

"I have thought about it. I have already planned to go back to San Diego. I have my family now and little Jonathan, not to mention Peppa. You can stay here and move on with your life."

"What about the gallery? We have spent nearly $8,000 to open it in two weeks. We already signed a full-year lease."

"We can break the lease. I'll open the gallery in San Diego."

"Fuck that, you'll open the gallery here. We both have a lot of money invested in it. Or you can buy me out."

"All my money is invested in the gallery. Where am I supposed to live?"

"You'll stay here until we figure something out. We just won't be together."

"Isaiah, that's not fair to you or me. I think it would be best for me to leave. The damage has been done. We both need time to heal."

"What about Michelle and the kids? What about my other businesses, and the people helping us with the gallery?"

"Why prolong the inevitable? We can end it now and move on with our lives."

"Is it that easy for you?"

"What do you mean, easy? I have been in love with you from

the first day I met you. I have never loved anyone the way I love you. And I probably never will again. I don't want to hurt you anymore than I already have."

He finished his drink in one gulp. "If that's what you want to do."

"I think it would be best."

Isaiah walked out of the kitchen.

# Twenty-Two

At 6:33 A.M., the phone rang. Nicole answered it.

"Hello?"

"Hello, Nicole, did I wake you, baby?"

Nicole recognized Isaiah's mother's voice. "Hi, Mrs. Mathis, I couldn't really sleep. How are you doing?"

"Oh, I'm doing fine. No complaints. You know I'm up at the crack of dawn. How you doing, baby?"

"Things could be better."

"Is that hard-headed son of mine getting on your nerves?"

"No, ma'am, it's the other way around. Are you okay?"

"Everything is fine, just fine. Where y'all been? I've been calling for two days."

"We went out of town. Did something happen?"

"No, baby, everything is fine. Is Isaiah up? I just need to ask him about something really quick."

"Sure. Just a minute." Nicole climbed out of bed and walked downstairs. She walked over to the couch and gently nudged Isaiah awake. "Your mother is on the phone."

"Huh?" he said groggily.

"Your mother is on the phone."

Isaiah sat up as Nicole handed him the cordless phone. "Hey, Ma, what's up? How you doing? Did you get the money we sent you? Nicole sent it two weeks ago."

"I'm fine, baby. Yes, I got the money. Thanks to both of you. Why didn't you tell me y'all were going out of town? Where did you go?"

"We went to California. Nicole's sister... niece died."

"Oh, I'm sorry to hear that. Why didn't Nicole tell me?"

"You know Nicole. She didn't want you to worry."

"You offer her my condolences. How did she pass?"

"A car accident."

"You tell her I'm going to pray for her."

"I will mama."

"Oh, I almost forgot. A business envelope arrived here for you two days ago. It has both our names on it. It has page seventeen written on it. You want me to open it?"

# ABOUT THE AUTHOR

Sean La'Mont is a California native currently residing in Stone Mountain, Georgia, with her husband, D. Muench. Though her writing appeared in Ebony magazine in June 2008, this is her debut as a novelist. She is known nationally for her charcoal portrait art. Art lovers are encouraged to visit her websites. Reach out to her: slamoont@yahoo.com

**www.slo10.com**
**www.slo24.com**

# ACKNOWLEDGMENTS

To my mother Veronica, words will never express the depth of love I feel for you. The person I am today has been solely based on you. You are the inspiration for my illusion, my character, my business savvy, my work ethic, my values, the very core of my being. You continue to be so awesome, I never felt I needed a father. I remember you being front row and center at my very first performance of Tom Sawyer in the sixth grade; and selling my artwork at various art festivals today. Thank you so much for not only loving me, but for supporting me in all I do.

To beautiful sisters: Rosalyn Michelle, and Kimberly Nicole (thanks again for our names, Mom). I want to thank you both for loving me for me and for giving me all of my beautiful nieces and nephews (my children): Razee, may you rest in peace; Son Mi, Kenneth, Corean, Jakari, Antonio, and Kyla. You all give meaning to my life. Uncle Sean Loves Youflflflfl

To my entire family: Grandparents, may you rest in peace; Aunts, Uncles, Cousins, Second Cousins, and

Aunt Laura. Thank you all for believing in me, especially you Uncle Hashbone, rest in peace.

To my adoptive family, The Hawkins, and The Moore's, you were there for me when I had no one else. Thank you for all the loveflflfl

To my best friend Anthony Joseph Williams, it is because of you that I am an artist. You recognized the gift inside of me, rest in peace my friend. How I miss you...

To my former significant others, you know who you are, who assisted along the way, thank you.

To David, if not for you, this book would have never been a reality!

To my true friends: Frank, my son, Mose', my other son (rest in peace); Miss Barbara-Anne, I miss you girl. You were there from the beginning (rest in peace). Brad- ford, Oley (rest in peace), Miss CoCo (rest in peace). Fa'ana, my Samoan sister (rest in peace), Miss Taylor, Caprice, Marvell, and Sherhonda. Thank you all for being you.

A special thanks to my niece and nephew, Corean (rest in peace) and Son Mi, for their written contributions to this book. And a shout-out to Bradford for helping me keep Isaiah real.

To the Clubs, The Palace (Andre), Traxx (Phillip), and the best drag show in America, 'Stars of the Century'- thank you for giving me my first break in Atlanta.

To Raymond Duke and the entire staff of Black Gay Pride Atlanta, thank you for offering me a home to showcase my gifts.

For everyone who has supported me by purchasing Sean La'Mont Original Artwork and books, I thank you with all my heart.

May GOD Bless You All. Love always, Sean

## ALSO BY SEAN LA'MONT

**The Truth Kills**

**The Truth Revealed**

**The Final Truth**

**MBISHIRI-The Journey of Benjamin**

**WHIN-What Happened in Nevada**

**Mr. Charlie!**

**Karma**

**Miss Destiny**